Bordy

Bordy

by
ROBERT McKAY

THOMAS NELSON INC., PUBLISHERS
Nashville   *New York*

First edition

Library of Congress Cataloging in Publication Data
McKay, Robert.
  Bordy.
  SUMMARY: Just out of school, a young boy faces an uncertain future unless the diamond ring he found and kept and the people around him can force him to make some decisions about his life.
  [1. Conduct of life—Fiction] I. Title.
PZ7.M1914Bo   [Fic]   77-23305
ISBN 0-8407-6509-6

To Ann,

and to Karen

A foolish consistency is the hobgoblin of little minds, adored by little statesmen and philosophers and divines. With consistency a great soul has simply nothing to do. . . . Speak what you think today in words hard as cannonballs, and tomorrow speak what tomorrow thinks in hard words again, though it contradict everything you say today.

RALPH WALDO EMERSON

Bordy

chapter 1

Last day of school. A bunch of the seniors were standing outside . . . talking . . . excited . . . maybe some of them a little sad, though no one was going to admit that.

Bordy didn't know how he felt. Jim McBride had just asked him how he felt about graduating, and Bordy had thought about it a minute and had realized he didn't know. It was funny. He had gone to school in this town for twelve years, the last four at Hull High, and now it was all over except for the formality of graduation, and he was standing outside the school for the last time, goofing around with a bunch of guys and girls he would never again sit down in a classroom with . . . and he really didn't feel very much of anything.

"I'm going to be a counselor at a summer camp up in Maine," Kathy Merton replied to somebody's question. "I really like working with kids." She looked at Bordy. "What are you going to do this summer?"

"I don't know yet." Bordy shrugged. "Get some kind of a job, I guess."

"Why don't you think about college?" Kathy said. "At least try for a scholarship or student loan or something."

"I don't wanta go to college," Bordy said patiently. "We already talked about that a hundred times in guidance class. Just because you wanta go to college doesn't mean everybody else does."

"Yeah, but Kathy's right in a way," Jim McBride spoke up. "Look at all that stuff Mr. Carroll was showing us about how tough it is for a high school graduate without any special skills."

"I know. I know. I've heard it a hundred times," Bordy said. "But I'm sick of school. Can't anybody understand that? I don't like to study. I don't even like to read books. I hate algebra. I never would've passed English in a thousand years if old Peabody hadn't decided she wanted to make room for some other dumbhead. Now what in hell would I want to go to college for?"

"But you don't have to go to college," Jim said. "Why not a tech school like me? Electronics or something. Auto mechanics—that's where the money is."

Bordy didn't answer. He was looking at Kathy. They had gone together last year. It had been all right for a while, and then for no reason he could ever find had just kind of faded away into nothing. Kathy was okay. Pretty. And pretty uptight about a lot of things. She was always looking ahead five or six years till she could get her M.S.W., whatever that was, and be a real social worker. Which was all right, too, Bordy guessed. But

10

not for him. He wanted to start living his life now, not six years from now.

"I just don't understand you," Kathy said, with a not of exasperation. "You're not a dumbhead. I think you could be almost anything you wanted to be. But you don't want to be anything. You're not even *interested* in anything."

"I'm interested in the Red Sox," Bordy said solemnly. "And the Celts and the Bruins. Maybe I'll go on welfare."

"Now wouldn't that be a great life!" Kathy was getting herself worked up. "Just sit around and loaf all the time and watch TV. And when you're forty have a big beer belly and not know anything except where the Red Sox are. Now don't tell me that's all you want out of life, Bordy Masterson!"

Bordy looked at her, grinning. "Okay, I won't tell you. But maybe I just want to have some fun, Kathy. If there weren't guys like me around, who would you social workers have to work on?"

Most of the group laughed, but some of them were looking at Bordy as though wondering if they were going to have to pay taxes to support him for the rest of his life.

"See you guys at graduation." Bordy lifted a hand. "Anybody want a ride?"

"We're all going to Ginny's house and listen to some records," Pete Fallon said. "Hey, I know what you mean about college, Bordy. I wouldn't go if they paid me. Not tech school either. But come on . . . relax. Let's go out to Ginny's and let the Zeppelin blow our head open."

"Nah. I'm goin' home and study the battin' averages."
He winked at Kathy, who gave him a cool stare.

On the way to the parking lot Bordy thought about
Pete Fallon. Pete's dad owned three lobster boats and
a piece of a seafood store, and Pete himself would rather
pull lobster pots than kiss his best girl. Or almost,
anyway. And when it wasn't lobster it was cod or
flounder or anything else that swam and brought a fair
price retail. It was a life Pete loved, and it was there
waiting for him, which made for a bit of difference between him and Bordy Masterson.

As usual Bordy had trouble getting his car started.
It was a '67 Galaxie, worth maybe half what it had cost
for registration and insurance. Bad car for gas and re-
pairs but the best he could afford and find. That was
one thing about living in Hull, Massachusetts. If you
wanted any freedom at all, you absolutely had to have
a car. Hull sat at the tip end of a long peninsula, which
made it only about ten miles from Boston across the
bay, but almost thirty by road if you wanted to drive.
And the bus service was so bad you could practically
say there wasn't any.

Hull was a funny town. Only ten thousand people
nine months of the year, and then over thirty thousand
during June, July, and August, when the summer
people came in. Full of big weird old houses built forty
or fifty years ago, when it was cheap to heat and main-
tain big weird houses. Many of them were closed completely nine months of the year. In the winter it gave
the town a forlorn, empty look, a look Bordy had grown
up with and was used to and had never even noticed
until he heard somebody from "outside" saying what a
dreary place Hull was in the winter.

Well, it wasn't winter now, and on this twentieth day of June, Hull was far from dreary. Driving down Nantasket Avenue toward his house on the bay side, Bordy had to brake a dozen times because little kids were always running out in the street without looking. And as he drove and used his brakes and kept his eyes sharply open, his mind was racing inside his head like a greyhound at Wonderland. And like the greyhound, no matter how hard it worked or how fast it ran, it never caught up with the thing it was chasing, and never really got anywhere except around in a circle.

When he got home his mother was watching a game show, his thirteen-year-old sister Yvonne was in her room playing the kind of rock records that made Bordy feel he was already getting old, supper was in the oven (smelled like macaroni and cheese) , and everything was just the same as it had always been.

Except for him. Everything was very definitely not the same as it had always been for him. Because he was out of school. Not just for today but for ever. It had been coming for months, so why now did it hit him so sudden and hard? The whole thing was crazy. He went upstairs to his room and stood staring at himself for a moment in the mirror. Bordy Gene Masterson. Nobody had ever told him where that first name came from. "Some nutty idea of your mother's," his dad had said once . . . and his mother had smiled off into the distance and said nothing.

So here he was, at age eighteen: five ten and a half, a hundred and sixty-seven pounds, black hair, blue eyes. Not good-looking and not bad-looking. An average guy—that's what he was. Maybe not even average. He didn't know anything that was worth knowing, couldn't do anything that was worth doing. Second-string linebacker and a fair third baseman who couldn't hit a curve ball. Good swimmer, which wasn't worth anything, except maybe to himself, and a pretty good hand with a boat, sail or power, but he could have been better if he had had a boat of his own. One thing he could do was run. Not fast but all day. Which wasn't worth anything either.

Jamming his hands in his pockets, Bordy stood looking out his bedroom window across the bay. Nothing to see. Lots of boats full of lots of people. But nothing to see.

You're bugging yourself, he said in his mind. School's over. You've been looking forward to it for a year, and now you're bugging yourself. Come on, man. There's a whole world out there. Get yourself together.

He went downstairs and sat beside his mother on the couch and watched the game show although he had absolutely no interest in it. His mother looked at him and smiled. She was a good ma. Still stuck back in the nineteen fifties with her Elvis records, but a very good ma.

Now his dad was something slightly else again. . . . And as the thought entered his head, his dad's car rolled into the driveway. "Hey, boy!" His dad rolled into the house. Somehow it seemed that whatever his dad did he was always rolling. "This is it, hey? Last day and all that jazz?"

Now that was one surprising thing about his dad. Dumb as he seemed a lot of the time, he had this way of knowing and remembering what was going on. His mother hadn't remembered that this was the last day of school. Smart as she seemed most of the time, his mother seldom knew what was going on right at the present moment. Sometimes she couldn't remember if it was April or June.

"Decided what you're gonna do when you get that diploma?" His dad polished off the last of the macaroni and cheese. "Whyn't ya let me put a word in for you with Ben Sykes, personnel man down to the warehouse? Me and Ben's pretty tight."

"Nah." Bordy looked at his plate. "I wanta try it on my own first." He looked up at his dad. "You know . . . I just wanta see if I can find something on my own first."

"So go ahead." Spreading his hands. "You can find somethin'. Waitin' counter at MacDonalds or somethin'. But the warehouse pays three bucks an hour to start. And you ain't gonna find many jobs like that floatin' around these days, boy."

"Yeah, I know. I just wanta give it a try, that's all." He stood up. "Excuse me." It was an old custom in his house to say that when you left the table. "I gotta go over to Jim's. We might go fishin' tomorrow."

"What's runnin'?"

"Stripers."

"You can fish all summer and never hit a striper," his dad said, leaning back in his chair. "Better leave 'em to the tourists."

Outside, Bordy sat for a minute in his car before trying to start it. What was it about his old man? He meant well, but he had this way of coming on all the time. No matter what you said, his old man always had to cap it.

15

No wonder his mother didn't have a hell of a lot to say, after twenty years of getting capped every time she opened her mouth.

For once the old Ford started first twist of the key. Maybe a good sign. He headed for Jim's house. They had things to do this night . . . but nothing concerned with fishing. They were going up to the park—Paragon Park, on Nantasket Beach—a real old-fashioned amusement park with a roller coaster and Dodg'ems and baseball throws and the whole carny bit. Only a couple of miles up the street.

He and Jim weren't going to ride the roller coaster, though, not unless it was absolutely necessary. What he and Jim were going to do was try to pick up a couple of girls. Summer girls. It was still a little bit early in the season, but some of them would be there—summertime girls from Brookline and Newton and Concord, floating free from Daddy's beach house, floating around with that summertime vacation freedom. Sometimes it turned out very, very nice. And sometimes it didn't turn out at all.

chapter 2

It turned out to be one of those nights when it didn't turn out at all. Oh, they met a few girls. Even took two of them for a ride on the roller coaster, which was a pretty expensive way to say hello. But nothing happened. The girls had to be home early. This and that. Always some reason you couldn't argue about.

"Maybe we're coming on too strong," Jim had said. "Maybe they see right away we're just trying to make out. Maybe what we ought to do is lay back and play cool."

"That's okay if you can do it. To me it's puttin' another game on top of a game. And I got enough trouble just playing one game."

"But it's a loser. We don't want to scare these girls, we want to get next to them." Jim shook his head. "Seems like you got to do everything the hard way."

That had been last night. Now it was the next day, after breakfast, and Bordy was sitting on the front steps, remembering. The hard way. Was that what it was? He didn't think so. The way it seemed to him was, you went straight at whatever it was you wanted. And if you didn't get it . . . well, you didn't get it. But it seemed to him that was better than putting up fronts and gaming people and sneaking around the back way or in the side door and pretending half the time that you wanted what you didn't want and you didn't want what you really did want.

The world was a very confusing place. The only thing he was sure of was that the straight-ahead way wasn't the hard way. It was the easy way. At least for him. But then, thinking about it, he began to doubt himself.

Because look at this: the main things he really wanted were things he never told anybody about. What he wanted most of all was a good life. And he wasn't even sure what that meant. He was sure of a few things it didn't mean. It didn't mean driving a delivery van for forty years like his dad and then taking your retirement and sitting around waiting to die.

Not that there was anything wrong in driving a van. What was wrong was when your whole life was driving the van and coming home and eating supper and drinking beer and watching TV and going to bed and getting up and driving the van. . . .

It was funny. Talk about not gaming, talk about being honest. . . . How about when he was talking to Kathy yesterday? Pretending to be honest, pretending to be cool . . . and all the time what he really wanted to say, not just to Kathy but to all of them, was more like: *Hey, you guys! I don't know what I wanta do. But I know I wanta do something. I want a good life. I want to do things that I like—and, yeah, that are good for other people too. But I don't know what. I don't think college can help me any. Not now, anyway. I envy you, with your plans all set up and your life sort of stretching out as far as you can see in front of you. But then on the other side I don't envy you either, because I think a lot of you don't know what the hell you're talking about. And I can't talk to you about what I want, because if I don't even know, then how could you understand? And so we just stare at each other . . . and there ain't nothin' happenin'.*

He stood up, stretched, went back in the house. "I'm gonna go look for a job," he told his mother. She was straightening up the living room, watching an early movie out of the corner of her eye.

"Already?" She looked at him, puzzled. "You haven't even graduated yet."

"Tomorrow. I just wanta get started, that's all."

"Well, I suppose that's a good idea." She frowned at the TV. "You don't want to work in the warehouse, do you?"

"Not especially."

She switched her gaze from the TV, looking right at him now, smiling, but with something behind the smile, too. "It just doesn't seem possible, Bordy. Through school and ready to go to work. I just don't know where the time has gone."

"Where it always goes, I guess. Down the drain."

"Oh . . . that's no way to talk. Time is all we've got. We have to make good use of it."

Sure, he was thinking as he got in his car, make good use of it. Is that what you've done, Ma? Twenty years gone by, your best twenty, and you don't even know where they went. And that's exactly what I don't want to have happen to me.

The man at the Hire-a-Teen Center in Quincy was pleasant but not very encouraging. "It's tough right now," he said. "Everybody out of school. Lots of college people looking for part-time work. If you want a regular job you'd do better at the State Employment or one of the private agencies."

"I don't want a regular job," Bordy said, deciding to be honest. "I just wanta earn some money as quick as I can so I can take a trip."

"Maybe one of those day-labor places," the man said. "They don't pay a whole lot . . . but then neither do we."

"Yeah. Okay. Well, thanks for—"

The phone on the man's desk rang. Bordy started to get up . . . then decided to stay. The man was talking, mostly saying "Yes," and "I see."

He wrote down an address. Hanging up the phone, he gave Bordy a surprised look. "This might be your lucky day," he said. "That was a lady in Cohasset. She wants her house cleaned from top to bottom. Sounds like it could be a fairly big job." He glanced down at the form Bordy had filled out. "I might give you a chance at it because it's close to your home . . . and you've got a car. Cohasset's hard to get to by bus. Are you interested?"

"You bet."

"Well, I'll have to check out your references before we can make it definite. But in the meantime why don't you go talk to her? Find out whether you suit each other."

Funny how things sometimes fall right in their places, Bordy was thinking as he headed back down Route 3-A toward Cohasset, which was right next door to Hull. It was a different kind of a town, though, a money town. Seemed like all the towns near Hull were money towns. Hingham, Cohasset, Scituate. Not that everybody in those towns was rich. But the towns were somehow more substantial, more solidly old-time New England. If you lived in Hull and were the sensitive, broody type, you could easily get your head screwed up thinking too much about Cohasset, Hingham and Scituate.

Well, never mind that, Bordy was thinking as he searched for the old lady's street. To him Cohasset was just another town, wealthier than Hull . . . and phonier. So you came out about even.

But still the house, when he found it, impressed him. It was big but not huge. Simple—the best kind of old-time New England house. White with blue shutters. Needing paint. A couple of acres of grounds, all overgrown and ragged. A barn out back—probably a garage now—and everything crying for care. When you looked closer, though, you saw that the decay was mostly on the surface. Underneath everything was still sound. Whoever had built that house had built it to stand up for a long time.

The old lady met him at the door. "You're Bordy Masterson? From Hull?" she shrieked at him before he could get his mouth open. "From that youth center or whatever it is? My neighbor recommended it. Said it was something of a gamble. You might get a dependable young person, and then again you might not. At least you won't get an old drunk. Ah, well, everything's a gamble nowadays, wouldn't you agree?"

21

All this in a single rush of words. Bordy had his mouth open now . . . and that was it. He was just standing there with his mouth hanging open, staring into the bird-bright eyes of this tiny old lady, feeling the energy come out of her, like you get from a five-year-old kid.

"I must say you *look* dependable," she went on without a pause. "And I for one place a good deal of store in looks. Not skin-deep looks, you understand, but the whole person I see when I look right into somebody's eyes. What do you think about first impressions?"

"I don't know. . . . I guess—"

"Well, come in, come in!" She gestured impatiently. "We can't stand out here and talk all day."

Numbly he followed her inside.

"First impressions aren't always right, I know that," she said. "But what else has a body got to go on in the beginning, that's what I'd like to know?" She peered at him as though hoping he might know. "I just made a fresh pot of coffee. Would you like a cup?"

"Uh . . . yeah . . . yes, ma'am."

"In the kitchen. It's the only habitable room in the house."

He followed her through a living room filled with ghostly lumps of dustcloth-covered furniture. Next to it was a dining room, large, sunny. The covers had been taken off the table and a few chairs, then tossed in a heap in the corner.

The kitchen was amazing. It had a tremendous fireplace big enough to roast a pig in—if you had a pig and felt like roasting it; a gleaming white refrigerator, not all that old, either; and rows of copper and aluminum pots and pans on the walls. It was the best kitchen Bordy had ever laid eyes on.

"Cleaned it up a little yesterday." The old lady spoke to his thoughts. "Place been closed tight for five years. Wonder there's anything left of it."

She poured coffee into china mugs, motioned him to sit down at the big round central table, then sat herself down opposite and regarded him with a kind of mild curiosity. The sudden silence beat upon his ears. He returned her gaze for a while, then looked away.

She sipped her coffee and hummed a little tune under her breath. When he looked back at her she was gazing absently out the window.

"Well, do you think you'd like to work around here?" Her bright, round, almost black little eyes were again peering at him. "Help me get the place cleaned up? They tell me the pay is two dollars and fifty cents an hour. Seems like a lot, but I suppose nowadays you have to expect it."

"I . . . uh . . ." Bordy swallowed. "Yes, I think I would. You mean just general cleaning up and so on?" He was trying to sound businesslike. At first he had thought she was crazy . . . at least a little nutty. Now he didn't think so. Two and a half an hour wasn't bad. And it looked like a lot of hours.

"My granddaughter's coming in tomorrow. But she won't be much help. Seventeen years old . . . no, probably eighteen now . . . and I doubt if she can make her own bed." The old lady laughed. Cackled. Bordy winced inside. Maybe she *was* a little nutty. "It'll be just you and me," she went on. "We'll have to work like dogs. Think you're up to it?"

Bordy let his breath out. "I think so. Can't start till day after tomorrow, though."

"Why not?" Pouncing at him . . . suspicious of people who can't start till day after tomorrow.

"It's graduation. I have to graduate from high school tomorrow."

"Oh. Well, that's good. Get it behind you." She extended her hand across the table. "It's a deal, then." Awkwardly Bordy reached out and shook her hand. And was surprised. No dry leaf there. Her hand was very much alive, and strong.

At the door he said, "What time shall I be here?"

"Eight o'clock too early for you?"

"No, that's okay."

"Good. I like to make early starts." She smiled. "Don't let my crotchety ways scare you, Bordy. We won't kill ourselves. I never did believe in a body killing himself with hard work."

"Me neither." Bordy grinned, suddenly feeling good about working for this old lady, dizzy though she might be.

Driving home, he realized he didn't know her name. He found the address card in his wallet. Mrs. Myrtle Beame—a nice old-fashioned name. It was going to be okay. He figured he only needed about three hundred dollars for the trip, and that place looked like it needed three hundred dollars' worth of work and maybe more.

As he hit Nantasket Avenue he began to whistle. "California, here I come." But not right back where he started from. No. Right *to* a place he could really start from.

chapter 3

Graduation Day. What could you say? Not a day like any other . . . and yet not the day you might have thought it would be, either. That's what Bordy was thinking as he stood in line to receive his diploma. The ceremonies were held outdoors, on the football field. The east bleachers were filled with parents and friends while the graduating class sat in folding chairs down on the field. So everybody except the commencement speakers was facing west. And one thing about Hull High's football field: you might not see the greatest football in the world played there, but if you sat in the east bleachers you did see one of the greatest views from any football field anywhere.

The field was located at the very end of the peninsula, surrounded by water on three sides. To the right, across the harbor, you could see the skyline of Boston, the mirrored tower of the John Hancock Building gleaming blue and silver . . . so near and yet in some ways so very far.

25

To the left, across Hingham Bay, lay Quincy and Weymouth, the shipyard cranes, and the huge gas tanks. And directly in front of you, only a few hundred yards across the tidal-rushing strip of water called Hull Gut, was Peddocks Island with its abandoned Army buildings and the old church and the hidden summer houses of the few rich people who now owned the island.

It was the only sentimental moment of the whole day for Bordy. He knew he would probably come back to that field and sit in those bleachers and watch the games and dream on the Boston towers . . . but it wouldn't be the same. Never again would the field be *his* field . . . his and Jim's and Kathy Merton's and all the kids' who sat around him now in the folding chairs under the early summer sun.

The moment passed. The principal handed him his diploma, a crackly roll of paper. Without thinking, he folded it and stuck it in his hip pocket. Later his mother would give it to him for putting a crease in it.

The rest of the day was blurry. Everybody wanted to have a big time, but somehow it never quite came off. Maybe we're trying too hard, Bordy thought once. In the end it seemed to add up only to too much music and too much talk and too much beer. He went to bed earlier than he had planned, and awoke earlier than he had to. And surprised himself by feeling absolutely great. No trace of beer hangover, no boring thoughts about what he would do with this first full free day stretching out ahead of him.

The old lady was waiting for him over in Cohasset,

with her old house to be cleaned, and money to be made. He didn't really give a damn about the old lady, or her house either. He didn't even give a damn about the money . . . except as a ticket to California.

And it was nice. He would go and do the job for the old lady, for Mrs. Myrtle Beame. What was nice was that though he would do the work and get paid for it, he didn't *have* to do it. Not like school. If he didn't feel like doing it, he could just say to hell with it, find yourself another boy. And there would be no penalties.

The old lady was waiting for him when he arrived. Not exactly waiting for him . . . working like a mad beaver, surrounded by pails of water soapy and clear, brooms and mops lined up against the dining-room wall like soldiers, two antique vacuum cleaners, and a jumble of hoses and brushes. It looked like enough equipment to clean the whole town.

"We'll start by washing down all the woodwork. Get the cobwebs out of the corners. Work down from the ceilings—I think that's the most efficient method. What do you think, Bordy?" She was wearing an old gray sweater with holes in the elbows and a pair of blue gabardine pants that must have come from a man's suit. They were both about five sizes too big for her. Around her head she had tied a crisp red bandanna.

"But maybe we should do the bedrooms first . . . I don't know." She cocked her head and peered up at him with those bird-bright eyes. "What do you think, Bordy?"

"Well . . ." He stopped and thought about it, just in case she really did want to know what he thought about it. "If it was me, I'd do the bedrooms first. So you'd have a nice comfortable place to sleep after working all day."

"You know, you're absolutely right!" She gazed at him in admiration. "Doing the downstairs first is just making a show for somebody else. Stupid!"

So up the stairs they went, carrying the buckets and mops and brooms. "We'll do my room first," she cried. "And then Tabitha's. What do you think about that?"

"I think you got the right idea." What a weird old lady. And yet, with all her funny ways, there was something honest and good about her. As they swept the ceiling and washed the woodwork of her bedroom, she chattered constantly. Half the time he didn't even listen, but that didn't matter, because when she really wanted him to hear she repeated herself three or four times. And she knew how to work, no doubt of that. She got down on her hands and knees and scrubbed the baseboards and pried into the cracks between the wide old pine planks of the floor.

At ten o'clock they stopped for coffee and English muffins and strawberry jam. Then they hung all the curtains and blankets out to air while they vacuumed the room and polished the furniture. To his mild surprise, Bordy found a certain satisfaction in doing the job right. At first he had been tempted to cut corners, or rather ignore them, but the old lady set quite an example, and her thoroughness was contagious.

By twelve thirty the room was finished, and Bordy had to admit it looked and smelled great. It was the biggest and best bedroom in the house, with two windows overlooking the front yard and a door that opened to a little porch on the side. Bordy was glad Myrtle Beame had taken this room for herself instead of giving it to her granddaughter.

She had told him during the course of the morning to call her Myrtle. At first it was hard; he wasn't used to calling rich old ladies by their first name.

"Do you want to go home for lunch?" she said as they came down the stairs. "Or would you like a grab a bite here with me?"

"Well . . ." He realized he hadn't thought about what to do for lunch.

"How about hamburgers? Cheeseburgers! I just love cheeseburgers, don't you?"

They turned out to be maybe the best cheeseburgers he'd ever eaten—on toasted buns with relish, and cold milk to drink and a cherry tart for dessert. "Store-bought but not too bad," Myrtle Beame said, nibbling the crust. "Not too bad a'tall. 'Course, if you're going to have lunch here every day, I'll have to take a little something out of your wages. Just costs. That's fair, isn't it?"

"Sure. You should take more than that."

"We'll see." She was gazing out the window. She had a way of sort of drifting off sometimes . . . probably remembering better days, Bordy thought.

The phone rang. "Oh, hello, dear! Yes, yes!" She looked at Bordy. "It's Tabitha!" she informed him, as though he were an old friend of the family instead of a newly hired hand. More conversation. "She's lost!" Myrtle Beame appealed to Bordy. "She's in Braintree and she doesn't know how to get here."

"Why doesn't she ask at a gas station?"

"She did. But she can't understand the directions they gave her."

"Well, Braintree's kinda hard to get out of. Tell her to try to get onto Route Two twenty-eight and keep heading east."

"You talk to her." She held out the phone. "She's all confused."

She didn't sound all that confused, Bordy thought after talking to her for a minute or so. She just sounded like a person who doesn't want to listen. In one of those Midwestern voices that clang so roundly on Massachusetts ears, she kept saying, "I know *that,* but. . . ."

With no confidence that he had accomplished anything, Bordy gave the phone back to Myrtle, who talked for a while longer. He was no longer listening, but was thinking suddenly of California and what it would be like trying to find his way around out there in a completely new and strange place.

"She wanted to know who that male chauvinist was," Myrtle Beame said, hanging up the phone.

"What?"

"That's what she said, male chauvinist."

Bordy looked out the window.

"We probably won't finish her room before she arrives." The old lady got up, found a pack of cigarettes on top of the refrigerator, sat down again. "Do you smoke, Bordy?"

"I used to. I quit."

"Probably a good idea." Myrtle Beame lit her cigarette, inhaled, let the smoke flow out gently through her nostrils. "I asked my doctor about it. He said that at my age it probably didn't matter. He's very much against smoking for young people, though. I guess I'm something of a fatalist." She paused, considering. "Whatever that means."

Bordy was half listening now. It was all right with him if she wanted to sit here and talk. Maybe if they sat around long enough the granddaughter would have to do her own room, which would only take money out of his pocket, he realized, and he wondered why he was starting to dislike this granddaughter before he even saw her. Because she had called him a male chauvinist? Nah. He'd been called that before, and worse. But mostly a year or two ago. The girls around Hull seemed to be easing off that whole male-female conflict thing.

"Tabitha's lived in Indianapolis all her life," the old lady said, startling him again with her uncanny way of speaking to his thoughts. "Perhaps the women's liberation movement caught fire a bit later out there than it did here."

Bordy shrugged. "I don't know. Seems to me that Hull's always about ten years behind Boston in a lot of ways."

"And Boston's fifty years behind the rest of the country in some things and fifty years ahead in others. One simply shouldn't generalize in such matters. . . . I know it and yet I always do it." She shook her head and made a *tch-tch* sound. "Why do people persist in doing things they know are stupid, Bordy?"

"They must get somethin' out of it." He eyed her curiously. "Were you ever a schoolteacher?"

"No!" She laughed. "Do I sound like a teacher?"

"Not like any I ever had. I was just thinking you might have made a good one."

31

She was smiling, all the million wrinkles in her old face becoming part of the smile. It made him smile, too, made him feel good. She might be nutty in some ways, but she was quite an old lady just the same.

They had gotten the second-best bedroom completely torn up—mattress off the bed, curtains down, windows half washed—when they heard a car in the driveway, and then a moment later the front door opened and a girl's voice called, "Grandma! I'm here!"

Myrtle Beame went tearing down the stairs. Bordy washed another window. He could hear their voices, both talking at once, full of exclamation points and little shrieks and bursts of laughter. After a while they came upstairs. Bordy had finished the windows and was scrubbing the baseboards. He kept his head aimed at a corner till Myrtle Beam said, "Bordy, I want you to meet my granddaughter, Tabitha Saunders. Tabby, this is Bordy Masterson."

Bordy stood up, turned around, and said "Hi." The girl said "Hello." They looked at each other, she with no great interest, Bordy with considerable interest. Tabitha Saunders was, to put it very mildly, a foxy, knockout, dynamite girl. She was a few inches shorter than he, slender, with short, curly blond hair, intensely blue eyes, and a full, rather pouting mouth. She was wearing jeans and a thin, silky blue shirt that would undoubtedly have gotten her sent home from Hull High School.

"I wish you wouldn't call me Tabby, Grandma."

"I've always called you Tabby."

"I know, but I don't like it anymore. Okay?" So sweetly appealing that a heart of steel couldn't have denied her, Bordy thought. "What a great room!" She gazed around, right through Bordy and out the window. "I know I'm just going to love it here!"

Then she focused on him. "Would you help me get my stuff out of the car? I've got just tons."

He glanced at the old lady. She returned his look with a bland eye. "Sure," he said, dropping his scrub brush in the bucket.

"Tons is close." Bordy surveyed the green VW Squareback parked in the driveway. The car was jammed to the roof with suitcases and cardboard boxes. "Not a bad car. What is it, a seventy-three?"

"Seventy-four. It's all right, but I think I'll get a Chevette in the fall."

"Me too."

She was opening the back end. "I'll need these suitcases upstairs, but I can't keep all this stuff in my room. I'll have to find out where Grandma wants it." She flew back into the house, not carrying any suitcases. In the end Bordy did ninety percent of the work, carrying everything upstairs into a spare room. Not that Tabitha wasn't willing to work . . . it just seemed that every time she got started there was need for another consultation with her grandmother.

By the time the unloading was done, Tabitha had opened four suitcases, hung some of her things in the closet, and strewn what looked like enough clothes to stock a good-sized store over the bureau, chair, and dismantled bed. Now she was talking excitedly to her grandmother.

"Do you know anybody who has a sailboat? Or a motorboat? I *knew* I should have brought my water skis. Is there any surfing around here? Is there a yacht club? Daddy said it's so hard to get acquainted with the right people in New England. Is that true, Grandma?" And on and on and on.

The old lady didn't know the answers to most of the questions. It wouldn't have mattered anyway, Bordy thought. Tabitha wasn't really interested in any answers but her own.

"Do you think it's hard to get to know the right people in New England, Bordy?" Myrtle Beame said when she could get a word in.

"No. But it takes a little time. Ten years or so."

Myrtle Beame laughed. Tabitha threw him a disdainful look.

"Guess we're ready to put the curtains back up," Bordy said, stepping over an open, half-emptied suitcase.

"Grandma, I want to go out and drive around town a little bit—see what it looks like. Is that okay?"

"Of course, dear." The old lady was frowning to herself. "Maybe we should eat out tonight. I don't have a darn thing in the house for dinner."

"Oh, that'd be fun!" The girl paused on her way to the door. "I'd love some seafood. Do they have good seafood restaurants here?"

"I really don't know. Do they, Bordy?"

"Joe and Nemo's over in Paragon Park has pretty good fried clams."

The old lady was gazing out the window.

The girl, eyes narrowed, glanced at Bordy. "Well, maybe I can find something else," she said brightly. "I'll be back in an hour or two."

"Yes, I'll have to admit she is a little bit of a snob," Myrtle Beame said as she and Bordy worked together hanging the ruffled curtains. "Poor thing . . . it's not really her fault. Her mother, now—even though she's my own flesh and blood—is a *real* snob. And her father's too busy selling automobiles to notice anything but his customers."

"Some kids have it tough."

"Now, Bordy! You're too good a boy to be mean about things."

"What makes you think I'm a good boy?"

"Never mind. I can tell. And I just have a feeling you and Tabitha are going to be friends."

Bordy grunted.

"You're good-looking, too. That's probably why Tabby was putting on her airs."

"Yeah, that's probably why. Poor thing doesn't want to get swept off her feet."

They finished the room in half an hour. It still looked like the tail end of a hurricane, but Myrtle Beame said they'd better leave Tabitha's clothes where they were. Maybe it'd make her feel more at home.

Bordy went to work on the hall. In an old iron vase on a drum table he found three one-dollar bills, tightly rolled. The old lady was in her own room, rearranging the contents of her dresser drawers. Bordy considered for a moment putting the money in his pocket. It had probably been in the vase, forgotten, for years. But then he decided, no, if he was going to be a crook, it wouldn't be for three dollars.

He gave the money to Myrtle. She was as delighted as if he had found a treasure.

"Here, you take this." She offered him a dollar.

"Nah. You keep it."

"Well, all right." She tucked the three dollars into the side pocket of her funny old pleated trousers. "But I'll apply it to your luncheon costs."

Later, driving back to Hull, he thought about it. Old tightwad. If she'd offered to split even, he'd have said okay. But then he had to laugh. She wasn't an old tightwad . . . she just had her ways. And Tabitha Saunders had *her* ways. And Bordy Masterson had his ways. And the way it looked right now, never the ways would meet.

chapter 4

The next two days on the job passed uneventfully. They had decided between them, he and the old lady, to work right straight through—Saturdays and Sundays, holidays if any—till the work was finished. " 'Course, either one of us can take a day off if we need it," Myrtle Beame said. "Work till you need rest, then rest till you feel like work again . . . that's my motto. How does that strike you for a motto, Bordy?"

"Great, if you can afford it."

"Well, both of us can afford it right now. Me because I'm old and rich and you because you're young and poor. Of the two, I'd take young and poor." She cackled. "But maybe you're not poor. Do you consider yourself poor, Bordy?"

"I'm broke, if that's what you mean."

"Being broke and being poor are not necessarily the same thing." She cocked her head and regarded him. "If I didn't want to sound like a fascist I would say that being poor may be largely a state of mind."

"Yeah. And maybe rich is a state of blind."

"Oho! Very good, very good indeed!"

They were waxing the dining-room table. It was fine old mahogany, glowing now with dark-red fire deep in the wood.

"Have you ever considered going into politics, Bordy?"

"Are you kidding? You practically gotta be a lawyer, and a fancy talker . . . and a phony on top of it. I hate politics."

"My husband was a politician." She gave the table-top a final admiring rub. "He wasn't any of those things. He had a way of getting to the point, of talking to people in language that made some sense."

"That doesn't sound like a politician."

"I know. Maybe 'politician' is the wrong word. Anyway, what are you planning to do with your life?"

"I don't have any plans. I don't believe in plans."

"You don't? Well, there are plans and then there are plans. Not having any plans is in itself a kind of plan. Wouldn't you agree?"

"Maybe. I never thought about it." What he was thinking about, right then, was Tabitha Saunders. For the past two days she had left the house about nine, and that had been the last he had seen of her. She had met some young people, the old lady told him . . . the kind of people she wanted to meet. Rich . . . membership in the yacht club . . . house on the shore. "Let's hope it's just a phase," the old lady had said. "Not that there's anything wrong in having money. Thinking it's important, that it can make *you* important, that's what's wrong."

Yeah, easy for you to say, Bordy wanted to tell her, but decided not to. Easy for rich people to say money was not important. If they wanted to go to California, they just up and went. Sure, money wasn't important if you had all you needed. Neither was air.

"Grandma! Grandma!" It was Tabitha, bursting through the front door, into the living room. "Julie Erikson said I could take her boat out by myself this afternoon. Isn't that wonderful!"

"You mean out on the ocean?" The old lady peered at her. "What kind of boat is it?"

"Not really out on the ocean. Just out a little way. Julie and I and her brother were going out, but now they have to go to Duxbury to meet an aunt or some dumb thing, so they said I could take the boat if I wanted to."

"They must be crazy." The old lady shook her head. "What do you know about boats?"

"A lot." Tabitha's face was flushed. Bordy was sitting on the floor, polishing the legs of a chair, looking at the girl. She was sunburned and windblown, dressed, but barely, in blue shorts and halter, pretty as your well-known picture postcard.

"Daddy had a boat for two years," she went on. "I used to drive it all the time."

"Oh, I can just see it!" the old lady was almost sneering. "Nice safe little boat on your nice safe little Indiana lake. Well, let me tell you, young lady: taking a boat out on this Atlantic Ocean is *quite* a different proposition."

"I know that! We were out yesterday. The sea was calm as a pond. Besides, they've got life jackets and a horn and everything . . . just in case you do get in trouble."

"Umm-hmmm. Life jackets and a horn aren't going to help much if you get in trouble out there. Now I don't set myself up as an authority on boating, but your grandfather was a great sailor, and he always said that nobody but a fool would go out alone on this Atlantic Ocean . . . and he didn't care how big a boat they had."

"Oh!" The girl was scornful. "Maybe that's the way it was in the old days, but yesterday there were so many boats out there that if you did get in trouble there'd be somebody to help you in about two minutes."

The old lady closed her eyes and rubbed her forehead, as though suddenly weary. Then she glanced down at Bordy. "You've lived here on the ocean all your life, Bordy. Do you think she should go out alone?"

"People go out alone," he said, knowing it didn't matter what he said. The girl was giving him one of those pressed-lips, narrow-eyed looks that women save up for muddy dogs and drunken strangers. "Some know what they're doing, some don't. Old lobsterman in Hull, Gus Carson, went out alone every day for forty years. Last winter the Coast Guard found his boat drifting ten miles offshore, everything shipshape, except no sign of Gus Carson. Never did find his body. It happens sometimes."

"Oh, thanks a lot!" The girl was furious. "Maybe he committed suicide. Did you ever think of that?"

"Can't say I did." Bordy went back to polishing his chair.

"Old lobstermen don't commit suicide," Myrtle Beame said positively. "What kind of boat is this, anyway?"

40

"I don't know. It's a pretty big boat, at least twenty feet long, and it's got flotation chambers so it can't sink, and a fifty-horsepower motor."

"Outboard?" Bordy asked, not looking up.

"Yes, it's an outboard."

"Well, that settles it," the old lady said. "You're not going out alone on that ocean in any outboard motorboat. Those things just aren't safe, I don't care how many people are with you."

"Fact is, some outboards are safer than some inboards." Bordy spoke directly to his polishing cloth. "Depends on the boat."

"Nobody asked you," the old lady said tartly.

"Ayuh." Bordy inspected his work with a critical eye.

"And stop playing that laconic New Englander role. It doesn't become you."

"Yes'm." Bordy tipped an imaginary cap.

"Grandma, please say it's all right. I'll be careful. And you know . . ." She hesitated. "I didn't have to come home and tell you at all. I could have just gone ahead and you wouldn't have known the difference."

"Unless the Coast Guard found your body," Bordy said.

"Oh! I wish you'd keep *out* of this. Why does he have to keep butting in, Grandma? He's supposed to be cleaning the furniture, not giving us advice on our interpersonal relationship."

"That's the way those Hull folks are," Myrtle Beame said. "It's their notion of how to be neighborly."

"Well, I don't need their neighborly advice. And I don't think you do, either!"

"Tell you what. I agree we don't need a whole lot of unsolicited advice. But I think I would accept Bordy's

41

opinion on the boat. So why don't you let him inspect it, and then, if he's willing to go out in it, the two of you can go out together. But I definitely don't want you to go out in that boat alone."

"I don't *want* to go out with him!" Tabitha was approaching tears, of rage or frustration or probably both.

"If it's all the same to you, Myrtle, I don't think I want to go out with her, either."

"Myrtle? He calls you *Myrtle?*"

"It's my name."

"Well, how come I have to call you Grandma?"

"You don't. Call me anything you like. Except Myrt," she added. "Myrt is a name I can't abide."

"I feel as though I'm going slightly insane. I came home out of simple courtesy to get your permission to do something I could have done anyway, and I run into all this . . . this *nonsense.*" She whirled and headed for the kitchen. "I'm going to have a glass of milk!"

"I really wish you'd take a look at that boat, Bordy. If it's unsafe she just shouldn't go out in it at all."

"Yeah, but you can't judge boats that way. Depends more on the person . . . what they do with the boat, and what they don't do."

"All right, then why won't you go out with her? Maybe you could teach her something about the dangers. You could regard it as part of your work . . . you'll be getting the same wages."

Bordy looked at her.

"Oh, I know, I know. That was the wrong thing to say. Look . . . will you do it for me as a favor? Because I'm worried about her going out on that ocean alone, and you're the only person I can ask to help me."

"Okay. If she's willing." He stood up. Truth was, he was curious to see the boat these rich kids treated so casually.

Tabitha, of course, was not exactly willing. But she finally decided that a boat ride with Bordy was better than no boat ride at all. So off they went, in her car, heading for Cohasset Harbor and the yacht club.

She made no effort at conversation, but neither did he. He was, however, very much aware of her presence in the seat next to him. Once when he looked past her at something on the side of the road she flicked him a sideways glance. For a second their eyes met. He felt a surge and a constriction inside him. This girl, this Tabitha Saunders—a summertime girl, yes, like the ones he and Jim were always trying to pick up at Paragon Park. So why all the strain? He settled back in his seat and tried to enjoy the ride.

chapter 5

The natural harbor at Cohasset was almost completely landlocked by high rocky ledges and was much more beautiful than any moorage in Hull. When it comes to harbors, however, beauty is far from everything. If you docked your boat in Hull you could, if you wished, sail all day and every day on Hingham Bay and never risk the open waters of the Atlantic. Or you could go through Hull Gut or around Peddocks Island and still find yourself in the comparative safety of Boston Harbor. Not till you slipped through the passage between the Brewster Islands and Point Allerton would you glimpse the limitless horizon of the ocean.

Sailing from Cohasset was a different story. Once you left that cozy harbor, you were instantly and totally at the mercy of whatever seas might be running, which was not to say that it was always or even usually dangerous. But it *could* be dangerous. Bordy had seen summer people, unused to the ways of the sea, take their funny little sailboats out on what appeared to be an innocently calm and sunny day, and then be caught suddenly in an offshore breeze and find themselves unable to stop their frightening drift toward the open sea.

With a power boat it was different . . . unless your power failed, and then it could be worse. The sea was too big, too strong, too unpredictable to fool around with. The difficulty was that people never learned to respect the sea until they had felt its force a few times. No use trying to tell them. They had to learn the hard way . . . and sometimes the lesson was learned too late.

The boat was moored at one of the yacht club's floating docks. Bordy winced when he saw it. Not a bad boat . . . for bay or lake. Not a good boat for the ocean. It was an eighteen-footer, what they called a bow-rider, a jazzy little boat with seats for too many people, a motor that could drive it too fast, and gunwales that could ship too much water, undoubtedly the exact kind of boat that Tabitha was used to playing around with on her Indiana lake. Flotation chambers, sure—that meant it probably wouldn't sink to the bottom. But a boat awash in fifty-degree water was not a boat that would sustain your life for very long. Fifty-degree water would kill you a lot quicker than any landlubber ever realized.

"Isn't it a beauty!" It was the first time he had ever seen Tabitha actually looking happy.

"How long have they had her?"

"Just a few weeks, I guess. But Paul Eriksen said it's a very dependable boat."

"Who's Paul Eriksen?"

"Julie's brother." Tabitha was impatient. She jumped down into the boat and stood looking up at him, hands on hips, her short blond curls lifting in the gentle breeze. "He goes to Yale, and he's had *lots* of experience with boats."

"Yeah." Bordy glanced at the sky and then at the weather signals flying from the yacht-club flagpole. Fair . . . light westerly winds. Should be no problems on a day like this. Maybe if they went out for an hour or so, the girl would relax and he'd be able to talk to her and make her understand the limitations of a boat like this. Inside himself he grinned. Who was he trying to kid? The truth was he wanted to spend some time alone with her . . . if necessary in a ten-foot skiff in a thirty-knot gale.

Getting out of the harbor was easy. Tabitha handled the controls, obviously proud of her ability to steer the boat, and of her rudimentary knowledge of "the rules of the road," the traffic laws that govern all boats from the smallest dory to the largest liner.

It was one of those June days the poets speak of: bright, warm, calm, absolutely mellow, and the sea was flat except for a long slow swell that reminded perhaps of some past and distant storm. In the sky a few cotton balls of cumulus promised nothing but continued fair weather.

Sprawling comfortably in the stern seat, Bordy relaxed and let his thoughts wander. There was really no use letting himself get excited over this girl—or even interested or irritated or disappointed or momentarily pleased by anything she might do or not do. She was a summertime girl, all right, but clearly not the kind that could be picked up at Paragon Park. She had her sights set on yacht clubs and guys who went to Yale.

She would pay no attention to anything he said or did, execpt possibly to laugh or mock. And that was okay. She had her ways, he had his. The world was full of girls, even a few who were prettier and sharper and foxier and cooler than Tabitha Saunders.

Tabitha was seated in front of him, amidships, controlling the boat with the automobile-type steering wheel and foot throttle that were connected by cables to the outboard. He doubted that she had any clear idea of the mechanics involved. Not that it made any difference, unless a cable broke. No use trying to instruct her anyway . . . let her learn from her Yalie boyfriend.

She opened the throttle a couple of notches. The boat was planing nicely now, hitting the swells with a solid little smack, throwing spray, skimming the surface of the water the way a boat like this was designed to do. Bordy looked over his shoulder and realized with a start that they were a good mile offshore. Minots Light was falling astern on the port side. He wondered if Tabitha knew anything about Minots Ledge, the terrible reefs that had claimed so many ships in the old sailing days, and that even today could still pose a very real threat to the unwary and uninformed.

"We're getting out quite a way," he called to the girl's back. She lifted a hand in response, but did not turn her head and did not turn the boat.

So to hell with it, Bordy thought. Let her go. They had plenty of gas on board, and with the weather like this there was no real danger. And there *were* several other boats within signaling distance . . . just in case something unexpected did happen. He knew he was being almost overly cautious, and he wondered why. Maybe there was something about this girl and the way she did things that awoke in him a need for extra caution.

He closed his eyes and lifted his face to the sun. Problems or no problems, it was great to be on the water again. One thing he was sure of: when he got to California he would live on the coast, probably somewhere around San Francisco, and the first thing he would do when he got enough money was buy a boat of his own.

He opened his eyes with a feeling of alarm. For a moment he couldn't remember where he was. A gray sky overhead. . . . He sat up abruptly . . . remembering. But a gray sky?

"What's happening?"

The girl looked over her shoulder, laughing. "You fell asleep. I guess Myrtle's been working you too hard."

"Hey! Where are we?" He looked around, feeling a surge of near panic. Nothing but gray mist. "Cut the engine!" he hollered. "You can't see twenty feet!"

"No. We've got to get in!" She didn't look at him. Her back, hunched over the wheel, was stubborn.

Bordy moved carefully from the stern to the seat opposite Tabitha's. "Listen! Cut the engine for a minute. Let me know what the hell is going on!"

Reluctantly she throttled back and shifted to neutral. The boat bobbed peacefully in a slight chop. "The wind's turning us. Now I won't know which direction I was heading." Her voice and face showed strain.

"Haven't you got a compass?"

She shook her head.

"Man! You can't steer a straight course in fog without a compass. Nobody can."

"I think I can. I was watching my wake . . . keeping it straight. Paul Eriksen showed me how to do it."

"Not in fog. It won't work. You'll just go in a circle." He held up his hand, listening. Far off he could hear a foghorn. Then another. But he couldn't be sure from what direction the sound came. "Look, I've been lost in fog before. It's very tricky, even *with* a compass. I think our best bet would be to sit still and wait for this stuff to lift."

"But maybe it won't lift."

"How long was I sleeping?"

"Not long . . . less than half an hour. The fog came so quick . . . I didn't even see it."

"That's the way it comes sometimes. We can't be too far offshore. Believe me, it's better to sit still. Barging around in the blind is just asking for trouble."

"But there's a wind . . . a little wind . . . and it'll be blowing us away from shore. I think we should head into the wind. If we go slow we'll be all right."

"Yeah. I know that sounds sensible. Trouble is, the wind may have shifted, and probably did. Fog like this doesn't usually come from shore."

"Well, I don't feel like sitting here, just waiting. Maybe if we go a little way we'll be out of the fog." Her mouth was set, stubborn and sulky. "I think we should *try* something."

"Okay." He shrugged. "Do what you want."

"The wind's coming from there." She pointed off the starboard bow. "That's the same direction I was

49

going in before." She put the motor in gear, and as the boat gathered way she swung it slightly to the right. "I'll go slow." She glanced at Bordy, her expression a mixture of triumph and uncertainty.

"We'll be all right," he said. "Just take it easy."

"Do you know what time it is?"

"No. Probably around three. We've got plenty of time."

The boat, wallowing a bit at such slow speed, seemed suspended in a pearly gray sphere. Tabitha looked back occasionally to check the wake. Bordy didn't bother; he was intent on whatever might come looming out of the mist ahead. That was another thing about fog: it played tricks on your eyes. Vague shapes were always appearing and dissolving. Also, the water was getting choppier, and the breeze felt stiffer. But it could all be imagination, he knew. When you got in trouble on the ocean, your senses grew superalert, magnifying every sight and sound and feeling. Not that they were in real trouble . . . yet. Fortunately they still had about twenty gallons of gas, but this big motor, even at slow speeds, gulped gas like a greedy baby.

"This is starting to bug me." Tabitha's voice was under tight control. "One minute everything was so sunny and safe . . . and the next minute we're lost in *this*. I don't see how people dare go out on the ocean at all if this is what you have to put up with."

"Well, it's pretty unusual for June."

She looked at him, then looked away. He felt the boat nudge forward. "Don't go speeding up now. That won't help any."

Instead of slowing down she gave it more gas. The

boat was rising on the water now, coming to planing speed. "Hey, are you nuts? There's bad rocks around here!"

"It's getting lighter ahead!" she screamed back. "We'll be out of it in a minute!"

She was on the edge of real panic, Bordy realized. He didn't want to take the boat away from her, but he positively couldn't let her keep going like this.

"Listen, Tabitha, you've got to—" The words died in his throat. Ahead of them, out of the fog, loomed a wall. The boat was driving full speed toward an unbelievably huge, black, blank wall. No! No wall. Bordy knew instantly. The hull of a freighter!

chapter 6

Tabitha screamed . . . spun the wheel violently to starboard. For a sickening instant Bordy was sure it was too late. A boat doesn't turn on its own axis like a car. A boat continues to skid through the water, in the direction it was going, for a considerable distance after the rudder swings the bow about. The tremendous ship and the tiny motorboat were now broadside to each other, no more than ten feet of water between them, and the gap still closing.

And then, just as it seemed the boat must surely crash against the side of the ship, the stern of the freighter slipped past. For a second all was calm, the frightening bulk of the freighter already disappearing in the gloom. In the next second the sea boiled up all around the little 18-foot bow-rider, and again Tabitha screamed in pure terror.

Bordy was already out of his own seat, grasping the wheel, wedging himself roughly into the seat beside the girl. *"Let go!"* he commanded her.

The boat pitched, yawed, spun in circles like a crazed bucking horse. Water came pouring in over the transom and over the bow. Bordy kept feeding it power. The boat banged against the turbulent water, hitting flat and hard like a toboggan flying too fast across bumpy ice.

"Slow down!" Tabitha screamed in his ear. *"You're going to crash us to pieces!"*

Bordy shook his head and pressed on. Then with a last convulsive leap, a last numbing smash, they were miraculously out of the frothing turmoil, back in the vast gray calm. Bordy reached for the ignition key, cut the engine. After the roar of the motor and the crash of hull against water, the sudden silence was as startling as a bomb.

"Had to keep going," he said. "The wake of a big ship like that can suck you down, tip you over, and stand you up like a bobber, if you don't keep plenty of power on." He could feel himself shaking. The release from tension, from fear, had been almost too fast. For the first time in over a year he wished desperately for a cigarette. "Good thing you turned right. Otherwise we'd have hit her, sure. And they never would've noticed . . . never felt us, heard us, nothing."

He was talking too much, but he didn't care. He grinned at the girl. Their faces were only a foot apart. She stared back at him, eyes so wide, pupils so dilated, it was like looking into two deep black holes.

"Hey! It's over. We're all right!"

She closed her eyes . . . opened them, focusing now . . . and started back from him. Or rather, she tried to, but she was pressed against the side of the boat and there was no room for retreat.

"My God," she gasped. "I thought we were going to drown."

"Me, too. For a minute."

"I've never been so scared in my life."

And that's when Bordy made a mistake. They were so close together. She was speaking to him openly, from the depth of their shared terror. All she wanted and all she needed right then, he realized later, was his presence, any human being's comforting presence. So what did he do? Yeah . . . pick this worst possible time to preach a little sermon.

"Probably be good for you," he said. "Nobody ever respects the sea till they've had the hell scared out of 'em."

Tabitha frowned and, though there was no room, managed to draw away from him. "I'm sure you're right. Grandma'll be glad to know I've learned a lesson."

"I didn't mean anything like that. We don't have to tell her anything."

"It doesn't matter. Do you suppose you could give me some room to breathe?"

"Oh, sure." He pushed himself up, stepped across the walkway to the other seat, and sat down, staring intently forward, at gray fog and nothingness. This girl . . . she could do it to you, all right. But why did *he* have to be such a numbhead?

"I suppose we'll have to sit here now till the fog blows away."

"No, we can't do that."

"We can't? Well . . . when I wanted to move, you said we should sit. And now when it looks like we should sit, you say we should move." She was tilting her chin higher with every word.

"It's different now. You know where we are?"

"Of course I don't know where we are!"

"I don't either, exactly. But I know one place we are. We're in a shipping lane, which means we're about three or four miles offshore. We gotta try to get back . . . or we might get creamed by another freighter."

"Oh!" Her eyes widened again. Her chin came down. "Do you know which way to go?"

"Nope. But I'm gonna make a guess. I'm gonna guess the wind shifted to the north . . . that's what blew the fog down . . . and I'm gonna guess it's holding there, maybe a little northeast. So I'm gonna keep the wind abeam to starboard and throttle down to slow trolling speed, about three miles an hour, and . . ." He shrugged. "Just hope for the best, that's all."

"But suppose the wind is from the south?"

"Then we're gonna end up six miles offshore, which isn't a whole lot worse position than we're in now."

"I suppose you want to drive the boat?"

"Doesn't matter all that much, but maybe it'd be better if I did."

She nodded, lips pressed tight, then got stiffly out from behind the wheel and stood aside while he took her place.

"Look, it's not important who runs the boat," he said, sensing that, for whatever reason, it was very important to her. "You were doing okay. It's just that maybe I've had a little more experience with the wind and so on, and right now I'd say we'd better take advantage of any edge we got."

"Oh, absolutely. I wouldn't want to take this responsibility anyway."

He glanced over at her as he started the motor. She was staring bleakly ahead. He half rose and tested the wind against his face. Maybe ten knots . . . picking up just a bit. He took a heading that put him a point or two into the wind. If his guesses were all right on the nose, he'd end up in an hour just off the three-mile stretch of sandy beach at Nantasket and Hull, with nothing to worry about except the breakers at Harding Ledge. But there was very little chance his guesses were all right on the nose.

"We really got to keep our eyes peeled," he said softly, to himself and to the girl. "We could, you know, run onto something bad any second."

"I don't understand these foghorns," she said after a few minutes, her voice not quite so tight. "It sounds like they're all around us. How can they be all around us?"

"Sound on the water's hard to locate. But they are sort of all around us. Let's hope the ones astern are ships, and that that one . . ." There was a ghostly booming hoot that seemed to come vaguely from the right. "Let's hope that one's the Boston Light."

They went on for a while without talking. One thing, he had no problem holding his heading, because the wind was freshening. He could feel it blowing sharp against his face. The chop was getting rougher. He felt that bad sinking feeling in his stomach. If they were heading out to sea, it could be very bad news. He was tempted momentarily to stop. But what good would that do? No good. This way they at least had a chance.

"I'm really getting scared again," the girl said.

"Nothing to worry about. I know that's the Boston Light horn now. Half an hour and we'll practically be on the beach."

"Are you sure?"

"Positive." He grinned across at her. She returned a smile . . . weak, but very definitely a smile.

And all the time, inside, he was cursing himself. Bordy Masterson, supposed to be a sailor, supposed to know about boats and the sea and how to stay out of trouble, supposed to know the signal, the distinctive pattern of sound and silence from the horn at Boston Light—but he didn't know.

And then he eased off on himself, realizing suddenly that there were probably hundreds of pretty good boatmen along this coast who didn't carry that kind of information around in their heads. They didn't need it, because they always had charts on board—charts that identified the lights and horns and bells and whistles. A lesson for him, one he should have learned years ago: never go out in a boat without a compass and a good chart.

He wished he had a watch. Funny how the fog seemed to distort his sense of time.

"How long d'you think we've been going?"

"Gosh, I don't know. Maybe half an hour?"

"Seems like it." He resisted the almost overpowering impulse to speed up, to find out as soon as possible whether they were headed toward New England or Spain. Was it getting darker? No, it couldn't be that late. But maybe the fog was getting thicker, piling up more heavily overhead. He told himself to relax, to stop straining so hard to see what could not be seen. The sea was not his enemy. Neither was the fog. The

57

sea and the fog did not care about him one way or the other, and the thing to do was ride with what *was*, and not fight so hard until there was an absolute need to fight hard.

From time to time he glanced at the girl. Mostly she was staring straight ahead, with the fixed gaze of a person who could walk smack into the side of a barn without ever seeing it. Once she met his eye and smiled that same wan smile. Poor Tabitha. She was out of her element now, confused and scared by forces she had never had to deal with. Bordy felt a part of him reach out to her.

"Are you cold?"

"No. No, I'm all right." She wrapped her arms around herself and shivered. "Isn't that silly? I really wasn't cold till you mentioned it."

"Hey, you can wear my shirt. I'm really warm."

"No!" She didn't look at him. "Actually, I'm not cold, I'm just scared. I don't like this fog . . . and it's getting so rough. . . ." Now she did look at him. "Don't pay any attention to me . . . just try to get us back."

"We'll make it. Don't worry." He didn't know what else to say. He knew what he'd like to say: *Come over here and sit with me and we'll keep each other warm and we won't be so scared and we'll have a better chance.* But he couldn't say it. God, it was stupid. They might be heading for the mid-Atlantic, or the slicing bow of a freighter, or the sudden horrible crash of breakers on a reef . . . and here they sat, the two of them, apart and polite, holding on to their apartness as though it were more precious than life.

And then he heard it—no mistake—under and over

the mournful foghorn bleats: that low, steady roar . . .
the sound of surf. Breaking on what? He didn't care. In
that first moment of listening he didn't care, because it
meant he had guessed right, and they would live instead of die. All he had to do was keep off from whatever the surf was breaking against, and wait till the fog
lifted. Everything was all of a sudden cool and nice and
no problem, just as he had said all along.

Baloney. He grinned. *You didn't know where you
were going.* I know, I know, he said to the other part of
his mind, but I made it, man, and that's all that matters.
Everybody's got a right to be lucky sometimes.

He cut the engine, turned to look at the girl. She
stared back at him, her face drawn in new alarm.

"What's the matter?"

"Listen."

She listened, without comprehension. "What is it?"

"Surf. We're near shore."

"Oh, God!" Instantly she began to cry.

"Hey, we're okay now." He reached across the walkway, wanting to touch and comfort her. Couldn't quite
reach her. Stumbled in his own mind on the urge to
leave his seat and go to her and put his arms around her
and rejoice together in their deliverance.

"Well, let's go in!" she cried eagerly, tears still stream-
ing but already forgotten.

"We can't . . . not yet. We gotta lay off here till we
can see where we are." He was full of tenderness toward
her. She was just like a little kid in some ways, scared out
of her wits one minute and then, as soon as she knew
she was safe, wanting everything to be totally good
again.

"Oh, no! I can't stand any more of this. Why can't we go in . . . if we're very careful? We might be right outside the harbor and never even know it."

"Yeah, and we might be standing right off a bunch of rocks and never even know it either." He got out of his seat, went forward to the space between the bow seats. He had seen the Danforth anchor lying there when he came aboard, and had then forgotten about it. Oh, boy! It was just lying there loose, tangled in its own line. Lucky it hadn't knocked a hole in the hull when they were banging around in that ship's wake.

He dropped it over the side, paying the line out two feet at a time, and found bottom almost immediately. They were in less than fifteen feet of water. What was the tide? Somewhere around low . . . certainly not high. The bottom was sand. He listened again, intently, to the sound of the surf. It sure sounded like waves on an open beach.

"I think we may be right off Nantasket Beach!" he called to the girl.

"Oh, fantastic! Well, let's go in. We can't get in any trouble on the beach, can we?

He came back and sat down again, opposite her. "Too risky. I'm not *sure* where we are. Look, take it easy now. We're safe here. It won't hurt us to wait a little longer."

"Oh my God. . . . You're worse than an old woman! Why don't we move in just a little bit? I bet we could *see* the beach."

He shook his head. "I don't care how mad you get. We're not moving till we can see where we're going."

"You're making all the decisions now . . . is that it?"

60

"When it comes to risking my life, I am." He took the ignition key out of the switch and put it in his pocket.

"You are really something else!" Her voice was high and ragged with scorn.

Bordy met her hostile gaze for a moment, then turned wearily away. It was hopeless. She had some kind of hatred for him that was over and beyond this stupid thing about pushing in through the fog. So to hell with it. He'd get her safely back to Cohasset . . . and then to hell with it.

"To hell with you, too," he said aloud.

Was he speaking to the sea or to the girl or to himself? It didn't matter. No one answered.

chapter 7

"She told me all about it," Myrtle Beame said. "Or possibly she didn't tell me *all* about it."

She and Bordy were working in the library—that's what the old lady called it, a small, comfortable room with a fireplace and deep old leather chairs and rather sparsely stocked, built-in bookcases. "I'm sure there used to be a great many more books here." She frowned at Bordy as though it might be his fault.

"One thing Tabitha didn't tell me . . . where were you when the fog finally lifted?"

"About fifty yards off the beach. Not a rock in sight."

"Oho! I'll bet she rubbed that in, didn't she?"

"No, she'd quit speaking to me by then!"

"Well, I'm sorry I got you into that fix, Bordy."

"You didn't do it. I did it. If I hadn't fallen asleep, none of it would've happened."

"Tell me the truth, Bordy, what do you think of Tabitha?"

"I don't have any opinions about her." He was impatient. "She's all right, I guess, in her own way."

"I believe she really admires you."

"Are you kidding? She hates me with a passion."

"Of course she doesn't hate you. I'll admit she does have her problems. You seem to make her uncomfortable in some way." The old lady puzzled about it silently for a few minutes. "All this modern concern with what they call female identity. I'm sure that has more than a little bit to do with it."

"You mean she hates men?"

"Oh, of course not! My goodness, Bordy, I thought you'd be more understanding about these things. Women *have* been at a disadvantage in this man's world for as long as I can remember, and I think you should understand that when you see girls like Tabitha trying to establish their own rights."

"I don't mind her standing up for her rights. I just don't want her walking all over mine while she's doing it."

"Tch-tch." Myrtle Beame shook her head. "There's something to be said on both sides, that's the dickens of it. But you men *have* had it all your own way for a long time now, you know."

Bordy didn't answer. The last thing he wanted right now was a lecture on the equality of the sexes. As he took the books down one by one and dusted them, the phrase stuck in his mind. Equality of the sexes. What did that really mean, anyway? As far as he could see, the sexes weren't and never would be exactly equal. Men could do some things better than women, and vice versa. What was wrong with that? Equal *rights* . . . sure. But having the right to do something didn't necessarily mean a whole lot. For instance, he had the right to be a linebacker for the Patriots . . . so what? The trouble with some of the red-hot women libbers he'd talked to was they seemed to think having the right was all they needed.

"If that's male chauvinism," he muttered aloud, "then I guess I'm a male chauvinist."

"Nonsense!" Myrtle Beame said sharply. "You're just overreacting to an overreaction, if you know what I mean."

"Yeah? Well, how're you supposed to know an over-reaction when you see one?"

"It's not easy." She peered at him, head cocked, bright old eyes black and sharp as carpet tacks. "I guess we all usually know after it's over with. But by then sometimes it's too late."

He thought about it as he carefully wiped a shelf clean and began putting the books back. He didn't want to admit she was right. It would just make life that much more complicated.

"Come on," she said, tossing her dustcloth on a table. "Let's take a coffee break."

As always, her coffee was so good it made Bordy sometimes wish he had never tasted it, because all the other coffee in his world now tasted like some poor imitation. Only this morning he had hinted as much to his mother, who was proud of the stuff she brewed in one of those tricky new coffee-makers. Her icy glance had discouraged him from elaborating.

"How do you make this stuff, anyway?" he asked Myrtle Beame as she poured him a second cup.

"It's not stuff. It's the best coffee I can buy . . . not the most expensive, just the best . . . and it's fresh ground for each pot, mixed with a broken egg including the shell, brought carefully *just* to a boil." She paused, smiling. "Good, isn't it?"

"Best."

She sat down again at the table and lit one of her unfiltered cigarettes. "Coffee like this is a thing of the past, Bordy. It's a *little* bit better than any other coffee you can get, and the reason it's better is because I pay attention to important details." Through her cigarette smoke she grinned at him like a nutty old turkey. "The lessons you can learn here, young man, may well be worth a good deal more than the wages you're earning."

He couldn't help laughing. "You may be right. They never did teach me anything about coffee in school."

"The lesson is not about coffee," she said sternly. "It's about—"

"*Grandma!*" Tabitha's voice came from the living room. A moment later she entered the kitchen, followed by a tall blond guy about Bordy's age, maybe a year older. "Grandma, I'd like you to meet Paul Eriksen, Julie's brother." Very formal. "Paul, this is my grandmother, Mrs. Beame." She looked at Bordy. "And this is Bordy," she said, making it sound like: "And this is our gardener."

"How are you." Bordy nodded.

"Hi." Paul Ericksen was easy, confident. Nobody offered to shake hands. He turned to Myrtle Beame. "And how do you like Cohasset, Mrs. Beame? Tabitha tells me you've only just arrived for the summer."

"Seems to have gone downhill a bit since I used to live here," the old lady said, lighting up another cigarette. "There was a time when Cohasset was considered one of the better places on the South Shore."

Paul Eriksen blinked, glanced at Tabitha.

"Paul's family has been coming here for *years,*" the girl said. "You may have known his grandparents."

"Unlikely." Myrtle Beame blew smoke through her nose. "I'm sure we were all insufferable snobs, but the fact is we seldom mingled with the summer people." She smiled gently at her granddaughter. Then she swung her attention to the tall blond boy. "Are you the young man who owns that speedboat?"

"Well, it's hardly a speedboat. Just a little runabout we use when the weather's good."

"Ah . . . and what do you use the rest of the time?"

"Well, we're really not into boats all that much."

"Not into boats all that much . . ." She shook her head. "I guess I don't know what that means. Do you know what that means, Bordy?"

"It means they just mess around with 'em." Bordy was suddenly enjoying himself. "When you're *into* something it means you think you know something about it, and when you're not into it all that much, it means you're just horsing around, you don't know nothing."

For a long moment there was silence in the kitchen. Bordy looked up, saw Tabitha staring at him in a kind of stunned pale anger. Her friend, Paul Eriksen, was frowning, not looking at anybody. Myrtle Beame was smiling innocently at anyone who wanted to smile back.

"We're on our way to play tennis," Tabitha said finally. "I just stopped by to pick up my racket. Come on, Paul." The two of them departed without farewells.

"I don't know why I *do* those things," the old lady mused to her coffee cup. "He's probably a nice-enough boy."

"He goes to Yale."

"Well, that's still no reason for my snubbing him. My husband went to Harvard and he managed to overcome even that disadvantage." She cackled to herself. Bordy wasn't sure he saw the joke, if it was a joke.

"Back to the salt mines," she said, getting up and putting the cups in the sink without rinsing them.

Two hours later, while Myrtle Beame was out of the room, Bordy found a ring in one of the old leather chairs. He had learned it was a good idea to investigate with his hand the deep recesses in the furniture before he attacked them with the nozzle of the vacuum cleaner Otherwise, he was always picking up hairpins and coins and pieces of broken toys that rattled alarmingly in the innards of the vacuum cleaner and made the old lady nervous.

The ring looked like a diamond, except that the stone was so big he was pretty sure it couldn't be a diamond. He held it in his hand for a moment, then slipped it on his little finger and admired it. The band was silver . . . or maybe platinum? He wondered. He knew little about jewelry, but enough to realize that if the band was platinum the stone might really be a diamond. It caught the light of the afternoon sun and reflected it back in a dazzle of cold fire.

Without thinking, without questioning at all what he was doing, Bordy put the ring in his pocket. When the old lady came back he kept his head to his work, the roar of the vacuum eliminating any need for conversation. He was thinking about the ring, though. What was he going to do with it? Steal it? Why didn't he take it out and say, Look what I found? If it was valuable she'd probably give him a reward.

He didn't take it out and say Look what I found. A couple of times during the rest of the afternoon he put his hand in his pocket and touched the ring. It was starting to feel like it was his. He was eager to get away from the house so he could take it out and look at it again. What he was going to do was just examine it and maybe try to find out how valuable it was. Probably it was just a piece of junk jewelry. So then tomorrow he could pretend to find it, and give it to Myrtle, and she'd be oh-ing and ah-ing and tell him some long story about who it used to belong to and so on.

Or maybe she'd show it to Tabitha and tell her how Bordy had found and everything. He shook his head in disgust. He was worse than some little kid, making up dumb stories. Tabitha wouldn't care if he found a ring, or ten rings. And furthermore, what did he care if she cared? He didn't like her, she didn't like him . . . they were different kinds of people, so forget about it, for God's sake. Forget about it.

When he got home that night he went to his room for a few minutes before supper, took out the ring, and looked at it closely in the slanting light of the western sun. Man, if that was a diamond! Its shape was a pointed oval, about the size of a big bean. Its color now seemed blue—an incredibly pure, icy blue. Was there such a thing as a blue diamond?

Then he remembered something he had read once or heard somewhere. Gingerly he reached out and scratched the stone against the windowpane. "Scratched" was the right word. Although he hadn't pressed hard, there was a definite scratch on the surface of the window glass. He picked at it with his fingernail. Definitely a scratch.

But was it true that a diamond was the only thing that would scratch glass? It was supposed to be true, he was pretty sure of that—which didn't mean a whole lot either, when he remembered some of the other things he had been told in his life that were supposed to be true. He'd have to find out more about it . . . yeah . . . go to the library, read up on diamonds.

And right then he felt his first flash of caution, or maybe fear. He wouldn't go to the Hull library. He didn't want anybody he knew seeing him reading a book about diamonds. He stood for a moment, considering. Then he opened his dresser drawer, took out a clean pair of rolled-up sweat socks, unrolled them, stuffed the ring in the toe of one, rolled them back up again. It was an old hiding place he had used over the years for forbidden cigarettes, extra money, different things he wanted to keep private.

Downstairs he heard his father come in, announcing his presence in the semibellow he used for a normal conversational tone of voice. Maybe being around Myrtle Beame had made him more critical of his own family's shortcomings. Not that Myrtle was above hollering, but the way she did it was different. The way she did most things was different. It was a difference hard to define . . . and impossible to miss . . . a quality. Tabitha didn't quite have it. Neither did that guy Paul Ericksen, what he had seen of him.

Ah, well, Myrtle Beame had her ways; the Masterson family had theirs. Bordy put it out of his mind as he bounced down the stairs, taking the last four in one jump.

"Hey, boy!" his old man said, coming into the living room with a beer in his hand. "How are you and Old

Lady Got-Rocks gettin' along?" It had turned into a kind of running joke, on his old man's part. Bordy had never said Myrtle Beame was rich, it was just something his old man had assumed—anybody who could afford to hire help for housecleaning was rich, period, and no argument.

Bordy shrugged and grinned. That was all his old man expected from him. Across the room his sister Yvonne had her head in a magazine. Out in the kitchen his mother was busy cooking supper. If he went out in the kitchen his mother would smile and probably ask him if he was hungry. It was an okay family, in a lot of ways a very good family. But not a family where there was a whole lot of what you could call real communication going on.

He went out in the kitchen. His mother for a change was sitting at the table instead of standing over the stove. She looked up and smiled.

"Bordy," she said in a low voice, "do you know very much about marijuana?"

"Huh?"

She put her finger to her lips. "Sh. We'll talk about it later."

He stood staring down at her, his mind whirling. Then he closed his mouth and said, "Okay," and went back into the living room.

chapter 8

"Later" turned out to be only a half hour after supper, when his old man decided this was one of the nights it would do him good to go out and quaff a few brews with his longtime buddy Jerry McQuade at the Dancing Dolphin. "The Dancing Dolphin" was a fancy name for a very unfancy bar and grill patronized by many of Hull's old residenters. It got its share of summer people too, of course, but they seldom stayed long or came back twice. The Dancing Dolphin was really a working-man's tavern in the old Boston tradition, which up until fairly recently had meant men only, and no loud-mouthed strangers. The loudmouthed regulars were suf-ficient unto themselves. At least that was the way the Dancing Dolphin had struck Bordy the few times he'd visited it.

Right now he was sitting on the front steps con-sidering various alternatives, as his teachers used to put it. Should he drive over to Jim's house? He hadn't seen Jim for several days. Maybe it was time they tried the

71

Park again and took a look at some of those summertime girls. Or maybe he should just stay home, save his money. But then how about the ring? What he should do, putting first things first, was drive up to Hingham, or even to Quincy—they both had good libraries—and find out something about diamonds.

"Bordy?" His mother came out of the house and sat down on the steps beside him. It was not a thing she did often. In fact, it sometimes seemed to him that his mother never came out of the house at all except to go someplace in a car. If was funny. Here they were, living in a house between the beach and the bay, in an area where other people spent thousands of dollars just to visit for a few months in the summer, and as far as his mother was concerned, they might as well be living in an Arctic wilderness.

"Bordy, I'm worried about Yvonne. I think she's smoking marijuana."

"*Yvonne?* She's only thirteen!"

"Sh. I don't want her to hear."

"What makes you think that?" He lowered his voice to a whisper.

"She's fourteen, Bordy. And she's very old for her age."

"But what makes you think she's smokin' dope?"

"I read her diary." His mother made a motion with her hands. "I know . . . I shouldn't read her diary . . . but I did . . . I think all mothers do. . . . I think they *should*."

"Oh, great. . . ." He looked at his mother. She stared back at him, her eyes round, apprehensive. It was the first time in his whole life he had ever looked at his mother and really seen her . . . as a person who got just as mixed up as he did, who wasn't really any *older* than he was, who lived in this same world that was hauling them all along, up and down and around the turns like the roller-coaster cars at Paragon Park.

"Do you ever get the feeling we're all nuts?"

"What?" She was looking at him with the same look.

"Did you ever read my diary?"

"You never kept a diary."

"Did you ever read my socks?"

"That doesn't matter now." She looked away from him, at their across-the-street neighbor, Mr. Morganstern, who used to be summer people but was now a year-rounder and seemed always to be either watering his lawn or doing something to his house.

"She said she's been getting high. A couple of times she said that: 'We got high—' and then that they did this and that. Now doesn't that sound like she's been smoking marijuana?"

"Well . . . I don't know. What was the this-and-that?"

"Oh . . . nothing much. Listened to records or went out to somebody's house or something. I mean there wasn't anything very bad about it. But getting high, Bordy . . . I know that has to mean she's been smoking marijuana. Now isn't that right?"

"Not necessarily. Might mean they just had a few beers or something."

"Oh, no!" His mother was emphatic. "I mean I know a little something about drinking beer and she wouldn't talk about it that way. Not at her age. I mean getting *high*. She wouldn't say it like that."

Bordy rubbed the side of his chin. He almost hated

73

to admit it to himself, but thinking about his little sister smoking grass was giving him a bad feeling. Why? Why was it all right for him to do something, and not all right for her? Because she was only fourteen?

"When I thought there for a little while that you might be smoking marijuana I didn't like it . . . I really didn't like it . . . but I knew it wouldn't do much good to say anything."

"You never told Dad?"

"Now what do you think?"

"Hey, Ma, you're okay, you know that?"

She smiled . . . kind of tired, kind of happy. "Pretty dumb but okay, huh?"

"I'm the one that's dumb." He grinned, suddenly embarrassed.

"Do you still smoke marijuana?"

"No . . . oh, maybe once in a great while. But I never did get that much out of it."

"What do you think about Yvonne doing it?"

He grimaced. "God, I don't know. Grass is a funny thing. Most people, I don't think it hurts 'em any. But some people get into it too heavy . . . it's all they care about."

"And doesn't it lead to other drugs?"

"I really don't know that much about it, Ma. But I don't think so . . . not for most people. I guess it's something like booze. You know, the old man drinks his beer and never gets drunk. Red Kincaid takes one drink and he's gonzo for a week. I guess you'd have to say it's always a risk."

"And it's worse for a girl, don't you think so?"

"Now that's something you're not supposed to say anymore. It's all supposed to be equal."

"I know. Maybe for some girls it is. Some women. I don't know. All I know is I worry a lot more about Yvonne than I did about you." She shook her head. "That doesn't sound right, but you know what I mean."

"Yeah." Across the street Mr. Morganstern was rolling up his hose. "I wonder if he's got any problems except watering his lawn and keeping the house painted."

"Everybody's got problems, don't worry." For a few minutes they sat in silence. "Would you want to talk to Yvonne, Bordy? She might listen to you."

"What am I gonna tell her? To quit smoking dope? To keep her guard up? She'll probably just deny it, anyway. What am I going to tell her . . . that I've been reading her diary?"

"Oh, I don't know." Again his mother shook her head. "I just wish it wasn't so hard for people to talk to each other."

"Well, you and me are doing pretty good right now."

"We are, aren't we? You know, sometimes I think I worry too much, and sometimes I think I don't worry enough. I've been a mother now for eighteen years, and I still don't know how a mother's supposed to act. Sometimes I can't believe I'm actually thirty-eight years old."

Across the street Mr. Morganstern was standing in front of his house, hands on hips, giving his premises their nightly final inspection.

"Look, I'll try to talk to Yvonne. No big-brother bit. Maybe just try to get a little friendlier."

"You know something? She'd really like that. She really looks up to you, Bordy."

He glanced at his mother and snorted through his nose. "You've been watching too many soap operas."

"That's all right. You can laugh all you want. But

there's something about you, Bordy. People just naturally seem to like you and respect you, whether you know it or not."

He stared out at the street. Mr. Morganstern had gone inside.

In a moment his mother got up, touched him gently on his head, and went inside too. He sat there for a long time, looking at nothing. Then he went up to his room, got the ring out of the sock, put it in his pocket, went back downstairs and out the door, got in his car, and drove to the public library in Hingham.

chapter 9

Myrtle Beame and Bordy were washing the kitchen windows. It was a slow job because the windows were made up of small panes, and the old lady's standards demanded that every corner be clean and streakless.

About nine o'clock Tabitha came downstairs and made herself a small breakfast of wheat germ and English muffins and grapefruit juice. Tabitha was not a coffee drinker. When she had finished eating she sat at the table for a while, paging through the *Boston Globe.* Bordy didn't look at her directly, but he could see her in the edge of his vision. She turned the pages impatiently, pausing now and then as an item caught her interest. Finally she laid the paper aside.

"Is there anything I could do to help, Grandma?"

"Well . . . if you feel like washing windows."

Tabitha said that was just what she felt like, so the old lady got a bucket, half-filled it with lukewarm water, and added a generous dash of vinegar. "You can use that paper," she said, indicating the *Globe,* "I guess we've all read it."

"But don't you use Windex or anything?"

"No need to. This is the way we washed windows when I was a girl and it's still as good a way as any. And a lot cheaper, too. Now watch." She crumpled a sheet of the newspaper in the water and vinegar, squeezed it nearly dry, gave two panes a brisk scrubbing, took another sheet of dry paper, and polished the glass till it shone. "Now how could you beat that?"

"Amazing!" The girl went to work. When she had finished her first full window, the old lady came over to check it out.

"Not bad." She pointed to a couple of places. "You've got to get into these corners a little better. On a job like this you have to get into the corners."

The girl nodded and glanced for the first time at Bordy. He met her eyes and grinned. She didn't grin back, but neither did she frown. She just went to work on her second window, digging diligently into the corners. He watched her for a second. She was wearing black corduroy shorts, cut off ragged, and a little yellow sleeveless shirt that left her middle bare. When she polished hard at the window, a part of her anatomy moved in a kind of reverse rhythm. Bordy directed his attention back to his own work.

"This is a really good way to wash windows," Tabitha said after a while. Myrtle Beame said, "Isn't it!" Bordy said, "Yeah, it sure is." And then the conversation sort of died.

Usually, when they were working together, the old lady talked constantly, whether to Bordy or to the world in general. This morning she was keeping her thoughts to herself. Bordy found himself missing her chatter. He tried to think of something interesting to say.

"Won't take long at this rate," he said.

"Not long a'tall," the old lady agreed.

Tabitha apparently felt no need to comment.

After they had finished the inside they did the outside. It was turning into one of the hardest morning's work Bordy could remember. When they had finished the kitchen windows they started on the porch windows. It was a big glassed-in sunporch.

"This house sure has a lot of windows," Tabitha said, when it was about eleven o'clock.

"Sure has," Bordy agreed.

Myrtle Beame said nothing.

Bordy turned to her. "Are you feeling all right, Myrtle?"

"Never felt better," she chirped, tossing a disintegrating wad of wet newspaper onto the growing pile in the center of the room. "Why do you ask?"

"I don't know . . . you seem awful quiet."

"Oh, I suppose I've got things on my mind. A body's got a right to have things on her mind, hasn't she?"

She wasn't looking at him. Neither was Tabitha. What was going on? It couldn't have anything to do with the ring, he was sure of that.

They worked right through till lunch. It was the first time since he'd been there that they hadn't stopped for a coffee break. Myrtle Beame offered no explanation, no apologies. Bordy was beginning to feel distinctly uneasy.

"We'll have to have cold turkey sandwiches," the old lady said. "That suit both of you?"

"Fine with me," Bordy said.

"Grandma, I've got a tennis date. I think I'll just go on over to the club and play before I eat."

The old lady shrugged. She was wearing a dress today, an old blue silky kind of dress that might have been bought thirty years ago for parties. Stained and strained now, it hung from her thin old shoulders like a memory of better days. For no good reason, Bordy felt his heart go out to her.

Tabitha was upstairs and down, out the door, and away in her car, so fast that she was gone before Myrtle Beame finished putting the sandwiches together. They ate, Bordy and the old lady, silently, not looking at each other. It was strange. There had never been any kind of constraint between them, and now all of a sudden they were strangers sharing the same table.

"Something's wrong," Bordy said.

"Um." The old lady flicked her eyes at him. "Too bad. I'm sorry I have to drag you into it."

"Into what?"

"Oh, Lord. I really don't know why I get so upset. Tabby's got her life to live. So have you. Why do I have to get so upset about things?"

"You don't usually."

"No, I don't usually. I put up a very good front for an old lady, don't I?"

"I don't know what you mean."

"Of course you don't. It's all right, Bordy. Please don't worry about it."

He ate his sandwich. The turkey was probably good. He couldn't taste it. "I . . . uh . . . I don't know what to say. But everything was going along so good . . . and now it's not. I mean I know it's none of my business. . . ." He stopped. Why was he doing this? The old lady's problems were her problems. Tabitha was . . . well, whatever she was. It was none of his business.

80

"I think Tabitha is taking drugs," Myrtle Beame said.

Oh, no! His mind stopped, on a pinpoint in nowhere.

"She was talking to that boy . . . Paul . . . last night. I was in my room, but I could hear them. I didn't want to listen, but I couldn't help hearing them." The old lady looked at Bordy, a full look for the first time all day. "They were downstairs. They weren't doing anything, just talking . . . louder than they knew . . . or maybe it's this old house. Voices carry. . . ." Her own voice tailed off. Bordy swallowed the last bite of his sandwich.

"They were talking about getting high," the old lady said. "Getting high. Tabby asked him if it was really good dope . . . something like that. *Dope,* Bordy. She's only eighteen years old and she's taking dope!"

"They were probably talking about smoking grass," Bordy said. "It's not dope. That's just a word some people use. Marijuana. It's no big thing."

"No big thing! Well, I beg to differ with you. To me it's a big thing. To me, that's taking drugs."

Bordy sighed. The turkey sandwiches had been giving him strength back. Now he felt very tired again. "I don't know what it is," he said. "The whole world seems to be going nutty about marijuana."

"What do you mean by that?"

"Nothing. Look, does Tabitha know you heard her talking?"

"No. I haven't said a word to her."

"She must have wondered what was the matter with you this morning."

"I'm sure she did. I just couldn't seem to act natural. Besides, I was flabbergasted when she offered to help. But then I figured it out after a while."

"Figured what out?"

"Why she offered to help, of course. What do you think we're talking about?" The old lady got up and did her thing with the coffee, egg, and cold water. "Sometimes, Bordy, you just don't seem to pay much attention to what I'm saying."

"I don't have a very high IQ."

She dealt him a sharp glance, then broke into a smile. "She offered to help because she wanted to be around you, that's why."

"No way!"

"Oh, it's easy to see. And I don't blame her. You'd make two of that fellow, Paul, without even half trying."

Bordy shook his head. "Your coffee's boiling."

"Darn!" She rushed to the stove, lifted the pot from the flame. "Boiling is *not* good for coffee."

"That guy seemed all right to me. How come you got so down on him so fast?"

"It's an instinct. He's a weakling. I can spot 'em a mile away."

"Maybe so, but you're way off the beam if you think Tabitha wants to be around me. I got some instincts of my own along that line."

She dismissed his instincts with a flap of her hand. "I don't know why it is. Men always think they know how women feel about them, while the truth of the matter is that most of the time they've got it absolutely backwards." She poured a dash of cold water into the pot to settle the grounds, looked back at him over her shoulder. "Have you ever smoked marijuana, Bordy?"

There was a name for this kind of thing, he had read

it somewhere. Déjà vu. Only that was where it just *seemed* as if you had lived through a scene before.

"Couple of times," he said. "I gave it up."

"Well, I know this is asking an awful lot, but the thought just occurred to me. If you'd be willing to talk to Tabitha, it's possible she might listen to you. At least it couldn't do any harm."

"Talk to her about what?"

"About smoking marijuana, of course! My lands, Bordy, you certainly do seem a bit dense today."

He put his face in his hands and peered over his fingertips at the old lady. "What do you want me to tell her, to quit smoking grass? That it'll rot her brain or something? Even if it was true, which as far as I'm concerned it isn't, she wouldn't want to hear it. She'd tell me to mind my own business, and she'd be right, too."

"But you don't think it's good for young people to take drugs, do you, Bordy?"

"It doesn't matter what I think. I mean it matters for me, but it won't matter to Tabitha or my sister or to anybody else. I don't know much, but I do know that. You can't *tell* anybody anything they don't want to hear . . . you're just wasting your time."

"That's where we differ." Myrtle Beame lit one of her cigarettes. "I agree it's useless to keep harping on little things, but there are certain important truths in the world that one must stand up for, and it doesn't matter whether anyone else wants to hear them or not."

"Well, I guess if that's what you believe, then you'll keep preaching. I just don't see where it does any good."

The old lady nodded, looking past Bordy, out the

kitchen window. Her face, though not exactly serene, seemed less troubled than it had a few minutes ago. "It's an old, old argument," she said, "and one we're not likely to resolve. Still, we have to keep at it, don't we?"

"You mean preaching at each other?"

"No. I mean, are you your brother's keeper? In the widest possible sense?"

The question startled him. "I don't want to be anybody's keeper. That's no good, thinking you got to be somebody's keeper."

"Of course not. Impossible anyway." She was dreaming out the window, beyond the sun-flecked trees and shady lawn. "My husband lost his last election because he insisted that in the long run the best thing for the most people would be a tax rise rather than a new bond issue."

Bordy glanced at her, looked away. He had no interest in taxes or bond issues or whether politicians should tell the truth. He had no interest in any of that stuff. All he wanted now, he realized clearly, was to finish this job, get his money, and head west, away from Myrtle Beame and her granddaughter, away from his own sister, away from all these problems people were always inventing for themselves.

And yet, as he worked alongside the old lady that afternoon, his mind kept flicking to an image of Tabitha, the way she had looked in the boat, huddled stubborn and alone against the mystery of fog on a sullen sea. And the way she had looked this morning in her ragged corduroy shorts and yellow shirt, doggedly washing windows, while inside her there must have been growing strain and discomfort over her grandmother's moody silence.

Had she really offered to help because she wanted to see more of him? Nah. Bordy rejected that idea totally. She was probably feeling a little guilty about not doing anything around the house, that was all. It wasn't hard to understand. The old lady was always looking for hidden meanings.

As he polished the last of the sunporch windows, Bordy let his thoughts touch, just for a moment, on the ring, the diamond—if it was a diamond. His reading at the library had given him no positive answer. Diamonds would cut glass, yes, but so would zircons and topazes and some synthetics. There were technical ways to distinguish diamonds from certain other stones, easy for an expert, impossible for him. Color was no guarantee of anything. There were red diamonds, and green, and yellow . . . and of course blue . . . blue-white . . . very rare, very, very valuable. This bit of information had been, in fact, the most discouraging. A blue-white diamond as big as the one he had found in the chair would be worth a great deal of money. Too much. It just wasn't possible anyone could lose a ring worth that much. The one saving possibility was that the diamond might be badly flawed. He wasn't even sure what that meant. But the book had quoted prices for a one-carat diamond: anywhere from three hundred dollars to three thousand, depending on a lot of things, like cut, color, and imperfections.

A carat was equal to a fifth of a gram, he had found that out. But how much did his diamond weigh? His diamond? Never mind. How much did it weigh? He had no idea. He didn't even have a very good idea of how much a gram was.

He stopped thinking about the diamond and tried to think about California. The trouble was, he didn't know all that much about California, either, except from pictures, what he'd seen on TV, and a few people he'd talked to. What he should do was get some books out of the library, read up on it. But it was hard to find what you were looking for in books. Take the diamond, for instance. He had learned a lot of pretty interesting stuff about how they were mined and cut and bought and sold, but he hadn't gained one solid piece of information to tell how much his own particular diamond (or nondiamond) was actually worth if he wanted to sell it. Damn a bunch of books, anyway!

"I really don't think those windows need washing twice," Myrtle Beame said from behind him. " 'Course, if it makes you happy, go ahead."

From the sunporch they moved to the basement. It was a mess, worse than he'd ever have expected. Barrels of dishes, old trunks, stacks of newspapers . . . everything going to mildew and rust.

"My God!" the old lady exclaimed, opening a trunk and shaking out a moth-eaten fur coat. "You'd think even a nitwit would know better than to store things like this in a cellar."

"I thought it was your house."

"It was . . . it is. But my sister Ruth and her family lived here for a number of years." She tossed the coat back in the trunk, slammed the lid. "When my husband died I moved into Boston, took an apartment on Beacon Street. This house was too big and lonely."

"How come you came back? I mean I know it's none of my business. I was just wondering."

"Why does anyone ever come back? Searching for happiness, I suppose. They say you can't go home again . . . but I don't know . . . I think you can, in a sense, and if you don't expect too much."

For some reason it made him uncomfortable, her talking about a search for happiness. If he ever got as old and rich as she was, he figured he'd just take it easy and quit worrying about things.

Tabitha came home about three. Paul Eriksen was with her. Bordy and Myrtle Beame were again in the kitchen, drinking coffee, talking about California. Bordy had told her he wanted to go to San Francisco. The old lady had been there, several times, though not in the past fifteen years.

"I was mad about that city when I first visited it," she said. "In fact, right after the war we seriously considered moving out there. But then we kept finding one reason and another to delay it, until we finally realized we didn't really want to leave Boston. It gets in your blood after a while, miserable winters and all. You live around Boston long enough and you find it very hard to leave, and I can't for the life of me truly understand why."

Tabitha and Paul Ericksen had been standing in the kitchen doorway, listening to the last part of the old lady's little speech. Bordy wondered why she had brought him home again—and why he had wanted to come—after the way Myrtle Beame had put him down the first time around.

"Would it be all right if I made some lemonade?"

Tabitha's voice was a bit louder than usual. "We got awful thirsty playing tennis."

"Of course, dear. Why don't you squeeze a few oranges into it? I think that's the best way to make lemonade."

The girl got busy with the fruit and the old-fashioned juicer. "Come on in and sit down!" the old lady hollered at Paul Ericksen, who was standing about five feet away. "How was your tennis game?"

"Oh, fine, just fine!" He flashed her a toothy smile, approached the table with confidence, pulled out a chair, and seated himself. "I couldn't help overhearing your last remark," he said, directing his full attention to Myrtle Beame. "My family has always lived in New Haven, and we feel the same way about that funny old town."

"Ah. . . ." The old lady held out her pack of cigarettes. "Do you smoke?"

"No, no. That's one vice I've never been tempted to acquire."

"Do you have many others?"

"Oh, not really." He laughed, glanced at Bordy, then toward Tabitha, who was working with her back to them. "Tennis . . . my mother would probably tell you I waste altogether too much time playing tennis."

"Ah. . . ." The old lady smiled, blew a neat smoke ring.

"Do you play?" He looked at Bordy.

"Used to. I gave it up." Why am I being a smart alec? he asked himself. This guy hasn't done anything to me.

A faint crease had appeared between Paul's eyebrows. "I don't know if you know it or not," he said to Myrtle Beame, "but Tab's got the makings of a great player."

"My goodness, Tab!" the old lady cried. "Did you hear that?"

The girl bent her head an inch closer to the juicer. Bordy was starting to feel bad for her. Why did the old lady have to keep shooting these needles in? She had a mean streak in her, no doubt about that.

"Is your father at Yale too?" Myrtle asked conversationally.

"No, no. Dad's in the insurance business. He's an alumnus, though. In fact," he said, nodding sincerely, "I might not have been accepted at Yale if Dad weren't an old Yale man. It just isn't fair, and it's one of those Ivy League inequities that some of us undergraduates are working hard to change."

"Well, good for you!" Myrtle Beame clapped her hands, spilling cigarette ash in her coffee cup.

Paul Eriksen beamed.

He can't be that simple, Bordy suddenly realized. She thinks she's gaming him, but this guy's a real cutie. He caught the Yale man's eye, and behind the deceptive grin saw the glint that told him he was right.

"Well, I guess it's time we got back to the salt mines." Myrtle Beame stood up, collected the empty cups, put them in the sink. "I don't feel like working anymore today in that musty cellar, so what say we take a look at the old barn, Bordy?" When he nodded okay, she said, "Maybe we can clear out a space for a car. I'll bet Tab would like to have a place to put her little car."

The girl whirled to face her grandmother. Her face was pale, her voice unsteady. "My car's never been in a garage in its life. Please don't worry about it."

"All right, dear," Myrtle said. "You children enjoy your lemonade."

89

On the way to the garage or barn or whatever it was or was going to be, Bordy kept telling himself to keep his mouth shut. None of this business was any of his business . . . and so on and so forth. But as his mother used to say, he might as well have been talking to the wall.

"Why do you keep needling her?" he said as Myrtle was searching through her key ring. "I mean she doesn't even know why you're doing it."

The old lady didn't answer. After two or three tries she found the key that opened the rusty padlock. Bordy tugged at one of the doors. It flew open with unexpected ease, confirming his notion that this whole place had been built to stand square for a long, long time.

Myrtle Beame stepped through the open door, and Bordy followed her. It was dark inside, after the bright sunshine, but from what he could see the place was nearly empty.

"This *was* a barn once," she said in a faraway voice. "My father kept horses here." She peered vaguely through the gloom. "The stalls were over there, behind that partition."

Bordy said nothing. He was glad the place was empty. The way things looked now there was nothing left to do but the cellar . . . maybe mow the lawn . . . a couple other little things. He should be done by the end of the week.

He looked at the old lady. His eyes were adjusting now. He saw her raise her hand to her mouth . . . her hand was trembling. "I know why," she said, her voice so low he could hardly hear. "I don't want to treat her that way . . . God knows! . . . but I keep on *doing* it." She shook her head wildly. The tone of her voice, and that gesture . . . In the dim light she seemed suddenly to have become a helpless young girl instead of the wise old lady he had always supposed her to be.

"I'd like to sit down for a moment, to collect my thoughts."

Bordy looked around, spotted a three-legged stool in a corner, brought it to her. She sat down with a sigh. He stood a few feet away, hands in his hip pockets, feeling awkward and impatient.

"The same thing happened to her mother," Myrtle Beame said after a while. "She was about the same age, only with her it was liquor instead of dope. She started drinking, running with a wild crowd, and there was nothing I could do to stop her. The harder I tried, the worse she got. Oh, not that she did anything so bad, but her values got terribly twisted. Good times, shallow people, money and the things it could buy—that was all she cared about. And she never got out of it. She married that fellow Saunders and she's spent the last twenty years in the most miserable kind of existence a human being can have."

"Well, I don't think you're going to help Tabitha any by treating her this way," Bordy said slowly, scuffing at the dusty concrete floor with the toe of his sneaker.

"I know. I know! But I just can't seem to help it. With her mother I tried logic and patience and understanding, everything I could think of, and none of it helped. She couldn't even hear what I was talking about."

"Well . . ." Bordy sighed. "That's what I was saying a while ago. You can't tell people anything."

"I won't believe that. I will not believe it! We have

to try, as best we can. We can't just sit back and let someone we love go to hell in a handcar."

"Yeah, but I think you might be exaggerating some. Tabitha don't look to me like she's going to hell, in a handcar or any other way. She's smoking a little dope, running around with a rich kid. That don't mean she's going to hell, for God's sake."

"You don't understand, Bordy. And I'm sure that sounds condescending and I don't want it to. It's not the actual *things* she's doing right now. It has to do with what she thinks is important, whom she admires, what she wants. All these little things add up to a big thing, and they're going to determine how she spends the whole rest of her life!"

"Maybe. I don't know. People can change. You don't have to get into a groove and stay there the rest of your life. I don't believe that."

"Of course, people can change. But look around you, Bordy, at the people you know. How many of them have you ever seen make any significant changes once they settled into a way of dealing with the world?"

"I don't know." He was trying to think. "A few. I know a few who did."

"So do I. A few who made marvelous changes. But the odds are against it, once you pass a critical point. I think there must be a kind of law of psychic inertia."

"What does that mean?"

"Well, if you start a ball rolling in a certain direction, it will continue in that direction unless some other force acts on it. And if the ball is a big heavy steel ball and it's moving very fast, it will take a great deal of force to stop it or even move it off its path. And I sometimes think the human spirit is like that heavy steel ball. Once it gathers enough momentum it just keeps right on going—it can't help itself—and it'll crash right through any stop signs or weak little roadblocks that are put up in front of it."

Bordy stood there, scuffing at the concrete. He could think of a lot of arguments. People weren't big steel balls. But then he thouht of Mr. Morganstern, and his father, and his mother, and Red Kincaid the boozer. Maybe not big steel balls, but rolling along just the same, and if you stood up in front of them they'd roll right through you. Not over you, not trying to smash you, but right on through you as if you were a patch of fog.

"So it comes down to the same thing," he said. "You can't change anybody. They're going to do what they want to do. So why worry about it?"

"You'd be surprised," the old lady said, cocking her head up at him, "at the influence a body can have. Sometimes when we least expect it. Because of course we're not big steel balls, we're human beings, and we affect each other in ways we don't even begin to understand."

"Yeah . . . well . . . Is there any more work you want to do today?"

"No." She stood up, back straight and shoulders square. "Let's call it quits for today. Been kind of a hard day, hasn't it?"

He hesitated for a moment, wanting to say something else, but then decided there wasn't any use. He didn't know what to say, anyway.

On the way out he glanced at the house. No sign of

93

Tabitha or her boyfriend, if he was her boyfriend. In the driveway the Yale man's car was parked behind Tabitha's. A tan MGB. Probably a graduation present from Dad.

Bordy's old clunker Ford was parked in the street. He had the usual trouble getting it started. God knew what it'd do when the weather got cold. Then he remembered he wouldn't be there when the weather got cold. Still, it wasn't a bad old car. It got him where he wanted to go and back again. It might get him all the way to California, and it might not. It didn't matter either way. If that ring turned out to be worth a lot of money, he might even buy an MGB for himself. Nah. He'd want a car you could stow some gear in. Maybe he'd get himself a dog when he got to California. Be nice to have a good dog to ride around with you.

chapter 10

That evening after supper he went to his room and took the ring out of its new hiding place—a crevice between the doorjamb and the wall in his closet. When he pulled up his window shade and let the full light of the western sun flood his room, he knew suddenly and without doubt that he was looking at a diamond.

What was it worth? God, that was the question. More than a thousand, for sure. Maybe two or three thousand. But what it was worth, and what he could get for it . . . that was another question. And how would he go about selling it? Well, he could make up a good story. He had inherited it or something. Boston was a big city, and a rich city. There must be plenty of people selling jewelry every day.

He tucked the ring back into its hiding place, went downstairs, found the *Evening Globe* scattered on the floor where his old man had left it, picked it up, and searched feverishly through the Want Ads. Yeah, there it was, under "DIAMONDS & JEWELRY:" "Gold and

Diamonds Bought for Cash." Another one: "Immediate Cash for Diamonds and Antique Jewelry." And then this: Expert Appraisal, Diamonds and Precious Stones, Certified Gemologist.

That was what he needed, an expert appraisal. He couldn't just walk into some store and try to sell a ring when he didn't know whether it was worth a thousand dollars or three thousand. They'd either call the cops or else cheat him out of his eye teeth. 'Course an appraisal was going to cost him some money. He knew that much.

"Whatcha doin'? Lookin' for a new job?" It was his old man, peering down at him through a cloud of cigar smoke. "Boy, you're jumpy as a rabbit in huntin' season."

Bordy forced a grin, casually turned the paper to another page.

"Might still be somethin' open down to the warehouse." He was fiddling with the TV. "I mean if you're interested."

"Nah. I appreciate it, but I just don't think I wanta work there." Why couldn't he tell his folks he was going to California? He was going to have to do it one of these days.

"Tell you the truth, I don't blame you too much." His old man grunted as he bent for the newspaper on the floor. "You got the TV section?"

Bordy found it in back of the Want Ads.

"Nothin' good on tonight," his old man said, almost before he'd finished scanning it. " 'Sox playin' tonight?"

"Yeah, but it's not on the tube."

"Figures." His old man shook his head in disgust.

"You don't blame me for not wanting to work in the warehouse?"

"Hell, no! If I was eighteen I wouldn't want to work there, either."

"But I thought you said—"

"I say a lot of things." His old man's eyes, pale blue and with no trace of beer fog, speared him across the top of the newspaper. "Half the time I'm just talkin' to keep from cryin'. Like everybody else."

Bordy stared at him.

"Workin' in a warehouse, drivin' a truck for twenty years . . . you think I like it any better'n you would?"

"I don't know. You never said anything. . . ."

"What the hell's the use of sayin' anything? I'm stuck with it." He lowered his newspaper and glared at the TV. Walter Cronkite was trying to tell him something about the Near East situation. "Shove the Near East situation, too," his old man said. "What the hell do I care about the Near East situation!"

"Why are you stuck with it?"

"It's hard to explain what happens. You don't even know it's happenin'. You start to work at a crummy job when you're young. You get married. After a while you get a raise, not much, but a little. You have a kid. You get a couple more raises. Now you got five years on the same job and you're makin' more than you could if you started out at a new job. Because you see you're not trained for anything, you don't really know anything, except how to drive a delivery truck . . . or run the lathe . . . or whatever the hell you're doin'. Those jobs all pay about the same. Only way you get ahead—they call it gettin' ahead!—is to stay with the same company, build up your seniority, your automatic raises . . . Keep your insurance and maybe your pension plan if they got one.

"By now you've got two or three kids and you find out all of a sudden that you can't *afford* to quit. It's a real kick in the can, that is, when it dawns on you for the first time that you're stuck with this crummy job maybe for the rest of your life just because you can't afford to take a pay cut while you try to get started at somethin' else you might like better."

"Yeah, but couldn't you go to night school or something . . . I mean if you really wanted to learn another trade?"

"Sure, sure . . ." His old man looked suddenly frustrated, baffled, in the grip of a dull helpless rage that could find no target. "It's possible . . . on paper it looks easy. Some guys do it, but most don't. I don't know why. You just seem to get caught in this circle, and time goes by and pretty soon it's too late." He stared at Bordy, his eyes wide and vulnerable. "I never tried to tell you what to do. You don't wanta go to college, that's okay. College by itself don't mean much either. But you might give it some thought, boy. I mean what you're gonna be doin' the rest of your life. Just driftin', lettin' things happen to you . . . feels okay when you're young. It don't feel so good when you wake up some day and your're thirty-three and you're trapped in some stinkin' backwater and no way in the world to get out of it."

Bordy had heard it all before, but not in quite these words, and never from his father. He had always thought his father accepted his life with something close to enthusiasm.

"Don't take it so serious," his father said, the old grin and twinkle starting to come back. "My life ain't been that bad. Fact is, it's been pretty good. I just get disgusted sometimes. At myself, you know. That's what it comes down to. Hey, don't ever tell your ma I was talkin' about being stuck with something. You know what I mean? Just the job and all . . . but she might not understand."

She might not, Bordy was thinking afterward. And then again she might. She probably felt stuck herself . . . maybe more than he did. If she and the old man could sit down and talk, be honest with each other, the world wouldn't fall apart if they both admitted they'd like to get a little more out of life. Maybe they could work something out together, try something new. They sure weren't too old, except maybe in their heads. Look at Myrtle Beame. She must be over seventy, and she went at things every day as if she had another fifty good years ahead of her.

He wished he could sit down with his parents and try to tell them. But he knew it wouldn't do any good. They wouldn't listen to some punk kid, especially their own punk kid.

He quit thinking about it and started thinking about the ring again. He knew what he was going to do: call Myrtle in the morning and tell her he had to go to the dentist or something. And then go into Boston and get that ring appraised. He couldn't make any solid plans until he knew what he had. And the old doubts were creeping in again. Just because the ring flashed pretty fire didn't make it a diamond. It might very well be a zircon or one of those synthetics he'd read about.

Next morning he left the house as usual, but stopped at a drugstore on the beach and called Myrtle Beame. He told her he had to take his mother to the doctor. No, nothing serious just some back trouble.

"Back trouble can be *very* serious," the old lady said,

and then she wanted to know if he was sure his mother had a good doctor. What was his name? "I forget. Listen, I'll be there as soon as I can." He hung up, cursing his own stupidity for not thinking things through a little better before he went into action. Especially when he was dealing with somebody like Myrtle. She was interested in details, he ought to know that by now. He'd have to get the name of a doctor. . . . Man, she might even call up his mother and offer some free advice—it'd be just like her. Well, too late now. He'd have to trust his luck.

On second thought, Myrtle had enough problems of her own right now. He didn't think she'd call his mother. The actual fact was, he was getting paranoid. He never had been a very good liar. So what he better do was get himself together and cool off before he flashed his might-be diamond at this Certified Gemologist in Boston.

The address was a jewelry store on Washington Street. There were three men in the store. They all looked at Bordy when he walked in. One of them kept on looking at him, so that was the one he approached.

"I have a diamond I'd like to have appraised," he said briskly. "I understand you have a certified gemologist here." He was surprising himself, how good he sounded.

The man behind the counter nodded, pushed out his lips, looked at Bordy over the top of his glasses. He had fat lips and a bald head, and shrewd, tired brown eyes. "Appraisal's ten dollars," he said. "Written appraisal's twenty. Guaranteed."

"Well . . . uh . . . you see I was left this ring by my

grandmother and I'm not even sure it's a diamond. I mean I wouldn't want to pay ten dollars just to find out it isn't a diamond." He smiled—a one-businessman-to-another kind of smile.

"If it's not a diamond we're not interested. Let me see it."

He took out the envelope he had put the ring in, because naturally nobody would carry a valuable ring around loose in his pocket. The jeweler held the ring between thumb and forefinger, looked at it. Then he stuck a black magnifying glass in his eye like a monocle, looked at it some more. He switched on a bright lamp, held the ring under it, studied it, turning it this way and that. "You say you inherited this from your grandmother?"

"Yeah . . . she died a few months ago and left me this ring."

The jeweler nodded. "Hey, Solly!" he hollered, startling Bordy. "Come over here and take a look at what this young fella's grandmother left him."

One of the other men sauntered over, stood beside Bordy, took the ring from the man behind the counter, studied it with his own magnifying glass. "Solly's our certified gemologist," the first jeweler said. "When you get an appraisal from Solly you got yourself an appraisal."

Bordy smiled. He was starting to feel a slight strain. The first jeweler hummed a little tune, nodding in time to the music, looking at Bordy all the while. Solly was tall and gaunt. Hunched over the counter, peering at the ring through his magnifier, he seemed to be trying to drill into it with the power of his gaze.

After a long time he straightened up, took the magnifier out of his eye, slipped the ring on his little finger down to the knuckle, held it out where the daylight from the street could hit it. The ring flashed like a crystal chandelier. Bordy was getting nervous. Anybody walking past the window would be hit right in the eye by that dazzle. Bordy didn't want any more attention. What he wanted was for this appraisal business to be finished. But he couldn't act too impatient.

"Well," he said after a while when it looked as though nobody else was going to say anything, "what's the verdict?"

"Verdict?" the tall gemologist said. "Is the ring on trial, maybe? What's with the verdict?"

"I mean is it a diamond? That's what I came in here for."

"Of course it's a diamond. You think I'd spend my time appraising a piece of glass?"

"Well . . . uh . . . what's it worth?"

"Are you interested in selling this diamond?

"No. I just wanted to get an appraisal."

"It's an old cut. Adds nothing to the value, let me tell you that." He was still wearing the ring on his little finger, moving his hand around so the stone caught the light from different angles. Then he took the ring off, laid it on the counter, rather carelessly, as though in the final analysis it had not quite measured up.

"A stone like that, it might have to be recut." He turned to the first jeweler. "Would that be your opinion, Mr. Latner?"

"You're the expert, Solly. That's what I pay you good wages for. This man makes more money than I do," he said to Bordy. "And I own the store. That's what the diamond business is these days."

102

Bordy smiled. It felt weak. "Well, if you could give me the appraisal. I mean I don't want to take up any more of your time."

"Time . . . what's time? I'm in no hurry. Are you in a hurry?"

"Not exactly, but I—"

"We could make him an offer," Solly said. "It's a gamble, a stone like this. But my opinion would be make a fair offer. Take it or leave it. A stone like this could present problems."

"I don't want to sell it. I told you, I just want an appraisal."

"So give him an appraisal," Mr. Latner said with a friendly smile at Bordy. "Can't you see the young fella's in a hurry? He came in for an appraisal, an appraisal is what he gets. Leonard Latner didn't build this business by arguing with customers, Solly. That's one thing you have yet to learn."

"A stone like this I can't give a quick verbal appraisal," the certified gemologist said, staring steadily at Bordy. "It wouldn't be fair to the stone and it wouldn't be fair to the profession."

"I don't get the point," Bordy said. Another customer had entered the store and was now talking to the third jeweler or clerk or whatever he was. What Bordy really felt like doing was grabbing his ring and getting the hell out of there.

"The point is a stone like this requires careful inspection for flaws. It should be taken out of its setting . . . the girdle may be chipped . . . the culet may be too large. In fact . . ." He picked up the ring, gave it a deep look with his spyglass. "Exactly." He laid the ring down again. "It'll take about thirty minutes. I can give you a written appraisal. Guaranteed. Otherwise, it's just a guess. I wouldn't recommend it."

"Look, all I want is a rough idea." Bordy appealed to the store owner. "That's all I came in here for, just to get a rough idea."

"So give him a rough idea, Solly. For ten dollars he's entitled." The owner spread his hands. "You got ten dollars, mister?"

Bordy gave him the money.

"A rough idea." Solly was shaking his head as though in pain. "A stone like this and he wants a rough idea." He lifted his high thin shoulders in a despairing shrug. "So all right, here's your rough idea." His voice changed, became the precise impersonal voice of a technical expert. "This is a marquise-style diamond, cut good to fine, color pale blue-white, clarity from very very superior to flawless, weight estimated four to five carats, retail replacement value difficult to judge accurately but would lie in the fifteen- to twenty-thousand dollar range."

Bordy felt as though he were standing naked on the beach in bright sunshine . . . with the temperature at thirty below zero. He was frozen solid. He could see everything very clearly—the gemologist's eyes boring into him like black diamonds and, off to the side, the gently smiling face of the store owner—but he couldn't move, couldn't speak, couldn't think.

"So for ten dollars it's not a bad appraisal." The owner's voice hummed gently through the ice.

"I . . . uh . . ." Bordy swallowed. He was back in the world again, or almost. He had never been in a twenty-thousand-dollar world before.

"Are you all right, mister?"

"Yeah. I . . . uh . . . I just didn't think it was worth anything like that."

"Your grandmother must've had a great sense of humor."

"Yeah, I guess she did." He took a long breath.

"Now listen. If you want to sell that stone I'd like to handle it for you. We can make a deal. Fair for both of us. Ask anybody on the street if Leonard Latner is a man to be trusted. They'll tell you. I'm a man to be trusted."

"Yeah, well, I've got to think about it. I just don't know yet."

"Sure you have to think about it. How many times in his life does a man sell a twenty-thousand-dollar ring? Of course you're not going to *get* twenty thou for it, you understand that. Replacement value at retail is one thing, dollars and cents when you go to sell— that's something else."

"Yeah, well, what would you think I could get for it? I mean if I do decide to sell it?"

The dealer shrugged, an elaborate, whole-body shrug. "Now that is where we move into another realm of the business. What you can get for a diamond depends on what some individual is willing to give you for a diamond. Makes sense, right?"

Bordy nodded. He reached out and picked up the ring, tucked it into the envelope, put it in his pants pocket.

"Why don't you leave me your name and address? A buyer might come in here tomorrow who's looking for exactly your ring."

"I have to think about it first." He was smiling and nodding, and moving backward with small steps.

As he reached the door the jeweler called after him, "Hey, mister! I know it's none of my business, but just out of curiosity . . . what did your grandma leave to your mother, a racing car, maybe?"

chapter 11

Driving back toward the South Shore he found it very hard to concentrate on what he was doing. Twice he came close to rear-ending a driver who was changing lanes. His mind was so full of the diamond there was no room for anything else.

Twenty thousand dollars. It was just too much. He couldn't grasp the meaning of twenty thousand dollars, what he could do with it, what it could do for him. So okay, it wouldn't be twenty thousand. More like twelve, maybe fifteen. Or say maybe only ten. Say that when he finally sold the ring for hard cash he got only ten thousand dollars. Well. That was a hell of a lot of money. He could live on it for a couple of years easy. Or he could buy a good used car and rent a nice apartment out in San Francisco and get a halfway decent job and live like a king. Maybe invest some of the money in a business or something. If he handled it right he could end up rich. Own his own boat . . . yeah, and women calling him up night and day, wanting to go for a sail . . .

He almost missed the Neponset exit and had to cut across two lanes. He cringed at the sound of angry horn squawks and a screech of brakes, but he didn't look back. He wheeled his 'Vette through Quincy in a dream of California mountains, swung his four-wheel-drive Cherokee into Weymouth, his mind's eye fixed on an endless sweep of Pacific beaches.

Then in Hingham he hit a traffic jam, summer tourists heading for Hull, Nantasket, Cohasset, Scituate, and came back with a thud to the old Ford clunker and Myrtle Beame's cellar, which still needed cleaning, and his sister Yvonne, who was fourteen and maybe on her way to a place she wouldn't like after she'd been there awhile.

He came back also to the diamond ring resting hot and heavy in his pants pocket. Well, he wasn't going to sell it around here, that was one thing he was sure of. He'd have to give his name and address, and the jeweler would probably check with the police to make sure the ring hadn't been stolen. Word would get back to his folks; one way or another something would go wrong. What he'd have to do was take it out west and sell it there. Maybe even get somebody to sell it for him. No, that was no good. He'd do it himself, and out there even if they were suspicious he wouldn't have anything to worry about. He'd get a California driver's license first and use that for I.D. No problem.

Except one. Not exactly a problem, just a bugging thought that kept trying to sneak through certain closed doors in his mind. Did the ring belong to Myrtle Beame? No, that wasn't right. Was Myrtle Beame the person who had lost the ring?

Maybe not. It could have been lost by one of her rich friends. Or by her sister, or one of *her* rich friends. Anyway, whoever had lost the ring was rich, no doubt of that. Which meant the ring had been insured. Rich people insured everything. Which meant whoever had lost it had already collected for it. Which meant that the only loser was the insurance company. Which also meant that even if he did give the ring back to whoever lost it—which he was definitely not going to do—that person would probably just stick it away in a bank vault, because even if she was rich she wouldn't feel like handing twenty thousand dollars back to the insurance company for a ring she probably didn't even want anymore.

So that part of it was no problem, either. Giving the ring back wouldn't be doing anyone a favor. He grinned sarcastically to himself. Giving the ring back would actually tempt the person who had lost it into becoming a crook. She'd gyp the insurance company for sure and then spend the rest of her life worrying that she might get caught. Even if it was Myrtle Beame. She didn't look *that* rich. And she was happy now with what she had. The ring was long gone, as far as she was concerned, so don't worry about it. For God's sake don't worry about that part of it.

When he reached Myrtle Beame's house he found Tabitha there alone. The old lady had taken the opportunity to go shopping and had borrowed Tabitha's car to do it.

"No kidding? I didn't know she could drive."

"Why not? She's no invalid. I found that out when I tried to keep up with her washing windows." They

109

were standing in the kitchen. Seemed as though ninety percent of the activity in that house took place in the kitchen.

"Wonder what she wants me to do?"

"I don't know. All she said was she wouldn't be gone long." Tabitha was prowling around the kitchen, opening and closing cupboard doors in an aimless search. Once she even looked up the chimney of the fireplace. "Would you like a cup of tea or anything?"

"Yeah, I guess so. I mean if you're gonna."

"Why not? Live dangerously, that's my motto." She flashed him a bright, mocking smile. Maybe more self-mocking than anything else, Bordy thought. She was different today . . . edgy but not hostile. It struck him again that she was a very complicated person, probably full of all kinds of doubts, which she tried to cover up by staying more or less on the attack all the time. But don't start thinking you can figure her out, he warned himself. Nobody can ever figure out anybody, not even themselves.

"Ever been to California?" he asked as she was putting tea bags in the cups.

"No, and I don't want to."

It stopped him for a minute. She had this way of saying things that could put a finish to a conversation before it ever got started.

"Well, I'm going out there," he said. "Soon's I get a little money together."

"Why?"

"What do you mean, why?" He frowned. "Why does anybody go anywhere?"

"Different reasons. I just wondered why California, instead of Georgia, maybe, or Wisconsin." She was pour-

ing the hot water, not looking at him. He studied her
. . . the fierce, concentrated way she did things, even
pouring water for tea. "It's funny," she said, putting
the kettle back on the stove and turning to face him. "I
came to Massachusetts because I think it has something . . . a tradition and . . . I don't know . . . a kind
of cultural atmosphere I think is important. And here
you are, wanting to leave it and go to California. . . ."
She shook her head, plopped down in a chair at the
table, took a somehow angry sip of tea.

"I never noticed too much cultural atmosphere in
Hull," Bordy said. "Or Harvard Square, either. To me
that's all a lot of crap."

"Well, I don't think it's all a lot of crap. I didn't put
it right. Cultural atmosphere is a sappy thing to say.
What I mean is, people who aren't totally wrapped up
in earning money and owning things."

"Yeah. The ones I've seen around Harvard Square
are more wrapped up in smokin' grass and livin' off
their old man's money."

"Wow. You and my father would get along great."

He took a big swallow of tea, and burned his tongue.
Why the hell was it, every time he talked to this girl
he ended up feeling like an idiot?

"I don't know about that. All I know is Boston's full
of phonies who are always putting down anybody who
works for a living . . . and all they're doing is mooching
off people and talking hot air. I get sick of 'em."

"You're really angry about something, aren't you?"

"Nah. I just don't like phonies, that's all."

"Neither do I. But you shouldn't let them bother you
so much."

He stared across the table at her. What was this? She

111

was the one who needed advice, for God's sake, not him.

"You ever smoke grass?"

Her eyes narrowed. "Why do you ask that?"

"I just wondered."

"I've tried it a few times. It just makes me sleepy. I don't like it."

"Good dope's all right. Wish I had a joint right now."

She shrugged, frowning into her teacup. "I think it's pretty stupid, wanting to drift off on a cloud to some place that isn't real."

"Well, you always come back. No harm done."

Her smile was thin and bleak. "Sometimes harm is done. I mean that's my opinion. But it's your life. You ought to find a lot of it in California."

"Dope or life?"

"Whatever you're looking for, I guess." She stood up. "I've got some reading to do. Grandma should be home any minute." She smiled, distant and polite, and left him alone in the kitchen. He sat there at the table, raging at himself. If he was trying to impress her he was sure doing a great job of it. And if he wasn't trying to impress her, then what was he doing? Acting like a twelve-year-old. No, a twelve-year-old would have more sense.

He sat there, thinking dull black thoughts, till Myrtle came home. "Well, well, well!" she cried, chipper as a springtime sparrow. "Did me good to get out of the house. A body should remember that: you have to get out once in a while, talk to some people, see how the world goes round. Otherwise, you get tangled up in your thoughts too much."

Bordy nodded.

112

"What's the matter with you? You look like you lost your best friend."

"Nah. I'm all right."

"Well, how's your mother? What did the doctor have to say?"

"She's okay. I guess he doesn't know exactly what it is."

"They never do, not with a back problem. I've got my own theory about back problems, but I doubt you'd be interested right at the moment." She bent toward him and lowered her voice. "Did you talk to Tabitha?"

"Yeah, we talked for a little while."

"Well . . .?"

"Well what?"

"You know what I mean. . . ." Whispering now. "About smoking marijuana . . . did you talk to her about that?"

"No." Bordy felt very tired, as though heavy weights were pressing down on him. "Yeah, I mentioned it. She said she doesn't smoke."

Myrtle studied him, head cocked, old eyes bright and curious. "Well, good for you!"

"Look, I didn't preach to her or anything. She just said she doesn't smoke."

"Do you believe her?"

"Yeah, I guess so. She was pretty righteous about it."

"Well, that's the best news I've had in a month!" Then she shook her head, frowning. "But I heard her with my own ears, talking to that fellow Paul about dope. I didn't dream that, you know."

Bordy stared at her silently. What did she want for two fifty an hour . . . a family counselor?

"All right, all right!" Myrtle Beame was undaunted. "It was very good of you to talk to her, Bordy. I'm proud of you!"

"For what?" He shook his head. "Whoever said talk was cheap, was right. Everybody's always talking and talking and talking, and then they turn around and *do* something, and that's what counts, not all the fancy talk about what they were going to do or should do or wouldn't do."

"True, true. But talking to the right person at the right time, and speaking as honestly as you can, from your heart, that's *doing* something, Bordy, and it can mean a lot. It can mean an awful lot."

"Yeah, I guess." But he was thinking: this is just more talk. She says something, and I say something back, and then she adds her two cents' worth to it. So it feels like we're doing something, but we're not. We're mostly just listening to ourselves saying things that make us feel better.

"Help me bring the groceries in and then we'll have a cup of coffee."

"Okay." He was going to tell her he'd just had a cup of tea, but decided not to. If she wanted to pay him for drinking coffee, fine. She could afford it.

Afterward they worked together clearing out the cellar. Bordy carried the junk she didn't want up the stairs and out to the street where the trash truck could pick it up the next day. He worked silently and steadily.

After his sixth or seventh trip up and down the stairs, Myrtle Beame said, "You ought to take a little rest, Bordy. Your face is getting red."

"Nah, I'm all right. It's good for me."

She pushed a wisp of hair out of her eyes and looked at him with some concern. "Do you feel like talking about it?"

"About what?" He felt a cold flash of alarm.

"Whatever's bothering you. Is it Tabitha? Your mother? Oh, I know it's none of my affair, but I just hate to see you keeping your troubles all bottled up."

"Who says I got troubles, for God's sake! I just don't feel like talking too much, that's all."

The old lady nodded, kept smiling. "It's one of my failings. I never know when to shut up. But you know that by now, don't you?"

"Aw, you're okay. I just get grouchy sometimes, that's all." He grabbed a bundle of newpapers under each arm, and as he started up the stairs he could hear her humming a little tune, the same tune she was always humming. He wondered briefly what it was.

chapter 12

When he got home that evening he walked into a blast of rock music that told him there was nobody in the house but his sister Yvonne, and maybe some of her friends. He went to the refrigerator for a glass of milk, spotted a six-pack of his old man's Knickerbocker, decided a cold beer was exactly what he needed. He popped the opener, thinking about his old man's philosophy that if kids wanted to drink, the place to learn to do it was at home. Sounded good on paper, but for some reason, for Bordy at least, it never seemed to work out. He wasn't that much of a drinker, anyway . . . a few beers once in a while were his limit. The funny thing was that he could enjoy a beer with the guys, or even alone, but when he tried to drink one at home under the deliberately nonwatchful eye of his old man, he always felt uncomfortable.

Right now the beer tasted great. He wandered back into the living room. The music from Yvonne's room stopped suddenly, as though she had lifted the needle in the middle of the record. Yvonne's room was on the first floor, in the back of the house. You had to go through the living room to get to it. Like a lot of the old houses in Hull, this one had probably been built by some individualistic Yankee carpenter with his own ideas about floor plans and ways to save space. Yvonne didn't like having to traipse through the living room every time she wanted to go to the bathroom, but whenever she complained about it, the old man just looked at her and told her to quit bitching, she was lucky to have a room of her own, and so on and so forth. Which was true enough, Bordy thought, but then again, it depended on what you were comparing it with. Somebody like Tabitha, say, would probably bitch if her room had only two windows and a private bath but no shower. And some girl up in Roxbury would bitch because her two little sisters had to sleep in the same bed with her. But would all three—Yvonne, Tabitha, and the girl in Roxbury—feel equally deprived? He had a sudden weird notion that they might. It wasn't so much what you didn't have as it was what you thought you were supposed to have. He turned the thought around in his mind a couple of times trying to decide if it meant anything.

"Oh . . . hi, Bord." It was Yvonne and one of her friends, Debbie Brendan. Bordy knew her brother Mike, a very nice guy, only a year older than him, and already turning into a boozer.

"I didn't know you were home." Yvonne was looking sort of wide-eyed.

"Where's Ma?"

"I've got to go." Debbie Brendan flashed him a

smile that almost made him flinch. What was she, fourteen? And giving him that kind of look?

"She had to go to the doctor. Mr. Morganstern took her."

"Are you kidding?"

"See you tomorrow, Yvonne." Debbie was at the door. "So long, Bordy."

He didn't look at her. "What's the matter with Ma?" Debbie let the screen door bang behind her.

"She burned her hand. She picked up a frying pan that was practically red hot. . . ." Yvonne caught her breath. "It was awful. I don't know how she does such stupid things!"

"Maybe because she was worrying about you." He hadn't intended to say anything like that. It just came out.

"Worrying about *me?*" His sister stared at him with an amazed look that was somehow not so amazed. "Why would she be worrying about me?"

He didn't answer. Just looked at her . . . really looked at her for the first time in a long time. Fourteen. . . . Unbelievable. She could pass for sixteen easy. Seventeen. She wasn't exactly beautiful, but she had a look about her. Guys would go for her, he knew that.

Her eyes slid away from his. She tightened her lips, turned to go.

"Wait a minute."

She looked over her shoulder at him. There was a wariness about her now, a kind of shutting out. He knew the feeling.

"Come on. Sit down for a minute."

She sat down on the couch, stiffly, watching him all the time.

He sat down in his old man's chair, then realized that wasn't too great a place to be sitting, got up, sat down again in a straight chair beside the TV. Why didn't he sit on the couch beside his sister? Funny thing . . . when you were going to *talk* to somebody (talk *at* somebody?) you didn't sit beside them, you sat across from them, sort of squared away, like a chess game, a contest.

"I was just wondering how everything's going."

"All right." She was inspecting the seam on her blue jeans, not looking at him. "Why are you asking that?"

"Just wondering. We never seem to talk anymore." She shot him a glance . . . dubious, suspicious.

"Hey, I'm supposed to be your brother. What're you so scared of?"

"I'm not scared of anything." Defiant now. "You never talk to me . . . and then all of a sudden you say sit down you want to talk. It reminds me of Dad."

"Oh, boy! Is that right?" He laughed. "Well, I sure don't want to sound like him."

She had collected herself into her own space now. She didn't believe him, he could see that. It made him angry.

"Boy, I don't know. I just want to talk to you for a minute and you get all uptight about it. What're you worrying about?"

"I'm not *worrying*. You're the one that's worrying."

He felt totally baffled. If you couldn't even talk to your own sister, for God's sake . . . ! He realized he was still holding the beer can, tipped it up, took a long swallow.

"I think I'm going to California."

"You are?" For the first time her eyes opened with real interest. "Does Mom know?"

"I haven't told anybody. I'm not even sure I'm going, but I think I am."

"That'd be cool. Wish I was."

"Maybe I'll take you with me."

Her face lit up for an instant. Then she ducked her head. "That's a lot of bull."

"Listen, Yvonne. Will you tell me something straight if I ask you?"

"What?" Again the look, closed off and wary.

"Do you ever smoke any grass?"

"Oh, that's it!" She jumped up from the couch, stood in front of him, hands on hips. "You're really sneaky, Bordy, do you know that!"

"No. I'm just sort of stupid, that's all."

"Mom told you to talk to me, didn't she?"

"Why do you say that?"

"Because. Just the way you did it." She stood in front of him, hands hanging limp at her sides now, her face a mixture of anger and despair. "I know she's been reading my diary. I wrapped a hair around it . . . different things . . . so I can tell when she's been in it. But she won't say anything. . . . No, she has to tell *you* about it."

"Better be glad she didn't tell the old man."

"Oh, I don't care! I don't care what any of them think. Always sneaking around, pretending things. I can't *stand* it."

"Well, that's the way people are, I guess. It's not just sneaking around . . . it's not knowing what to say." Listen to me, he was thinking. Who's the preacher now?

"I haven't been smoking any grass, if that's what you want to know. I just put that stuff in the diary to make

120

Mom mad." She was looking at him as if daring him to believe her.

"Why would you want to do that?"

"Because she hasn't got any right to read my diary, that's why. A diary is supposed to be *private*."

Bordy spread his hands. "Yeah, I know, but . . . you leave a diary around, you got to expect somebody's going to read it."

"Would *you?*"

"If I was interested enough, I would. What's the use of saying I wouldn't?"

"Well, I think that *stinks!*" Her face was flushed, twisted with scorn. "I think that shows you don't have any respect for *anybody*."

"Have you got a boyfriend?"

"None of your business!"

"Let's say you got a boyfriend. Let's say you're nuts about him but you're not sure how he feels about you. Let's say you're alone in his house for some reason and you happen to see his diary lying right there in front of you. Would you sneak a little peek or wouldn't you?"

"No, I wouldn't!" Really sneering at him now. "You're drinking that rotten beer and being so . . . so *superior*. You just make me laugh, that's all!" The sneer crumpled into a soundless wail. She gave him one last despairing look and rushed from the room.

Oh, boy. She was right, too. If he was going to preach to her like that he should've stayed in his old man's chair. He went out into the kitchen and threw the beer can in the trash basket.

After a while his mother came home, her right hand impressively bandaged. "Third-degree burns," she said.

121

"It's a new doctor at the clinic. Some kind of a Spaniard or something. He said it's going to heal very slowly. I didn't like him."

Bordy shook his head in sympathy.

"I guess it'll have to be TV dinners tonight. Your father'll be mad."

"Because you burned your hand? Come on!"

"No, but you know how he is."

"Look, why don't you just lie down and take it easy. We can heat up the TV dinners ourselves."

"Maybe I will." She was a little shaky, he could see that. "I just hate to have something like this happen!"

"Take it easy, Ma. You don't have to cook a big supper every night in the year, for God's sake."

"I know." She sighed, then looked at him with a different interest. "Oh, Bordy . . . did you get a chance to talk to Yvonne yet?"

"Yeah, a little."

"What did she say?"

"Not much."

"Well, I mean did she say she was smoking marijuana or not?"

"She said she wasn't."

"Well, I don't believe that. Not after what I read."

"Maybe she was putting you on."

"Putting me on? In her diary? That doesn't even make sense!"

"Look, Ma . . . why don't you just relax now? Your nerves are all strung out."

"Do you believe her?"

He made a motion with his head. "Look, don't be so impatient. You can't find out something like that in two minutes."

"She's smoking marijuana." His mother nodded rapidly. "I know she is."

He finally got her to lie down on the couch and watch the early news. Then his old man came home, and in five seconds had grasped the whole situation and was so amazingly gentle that Bordy had a crazy thought that his mother should burn her hand more often.

Yvonne stayed in her room till suppertime. When she came to the table she was pale and careful. Bordy knew she was wondering if anybody had said anything to the old man yet.

It was easy to be brave and sarcastic when you could do the whole thing with words, and at a safe distance. Who's afraid of the big bad wolf? Everybody, when the wolf's right there in the room with you.

The TV dinners weren't too bad. The old man grumped good-naturedly about his Salisbury steak, doing it in a nice way to make his wife understand what a great cook she really was. Bordy was starting to feel better. Instead of a disaster the supper was turning into a kind of nutty picnic. Even Yvonne was poking a cautious head out of her shell.

Bordy went to the kitchen to put water on for instant coffee. While he was filling the teakettle he heard somebody knock on the front door. A loud knock . . . knock . . . knock. For no reason at all he felt a chill. He heard his old man holler, "Come on in!" It was the way his old man always answered a knock on the door.

He put the kettle on the stove, taking his time. He heard a voice say, "Hate to bother you while you're eating. But is Bordy here?"

He knew that voice, but couldn't place it. There was a moment of peculiar silence in the other room. Then his old man called, "Hey, Bordy! Somebody to see you."

He went back into the dining room. The man standing by the other door, behind his father, looked as big as a house. All Bordy could see was the blue uniform. He had a horrible feeling that for the first time in his life he was going to faint.

"Looks like they finally caught up with you, boy," his old man said, grinning.

Bordy just stood there, staring at the policeman, waiting for the end of the world.

chapter 13

"That was nice of Steve, wasn't it?" his mother was saying, afterward.

"Yeah." The sick feeling had gone away, but he was still very unsteady inside himself. He glanced over at his old man, who was knocking down his second or third beer since supper. The three of them were sitting in the living room. The evening news had come and gone, with Roger Mudd filling in for Walter Cronkite. The Middle East situation seemed about the same.

"One thing about living in a small town," his old man said. "The cops take a personal interest. Lose a plate in Boston, forget it."

Somebody had found Bordy's license plate in the street and turned it in at the police station. He must have lost it this morning. He had driven to Boston and back with no rear plate, and nobody had noticed. Steve McGovern had checked it out with the Registry, learned it was his, and had then been nice enough to stop by at the end of his shift to deliver it. Just a good friendly neighborhood cop, with no present interest at all in diamond rings.

"You know, you really looked like you thought you were going to jail," his mother said. "You were pale as a ghost."

Bordy tried a grin. "I guess cops make me nervous. They're usually bad news."

"Now that's one of the things about this generation gap," his old man said. "When I was a kid we looked up to cops. We didn't hate 'em and we weren't scared of 'em. This thing today now where everybody's takin' cracks at the police all the time . . ." He shook his head in disgust, tipped up his beer can, left the sentence hanging.

Bordy wondered for the thousandth time how his old man could be so smart in some ways and so stupid in others. This thing about hating cops. It might be part of the generation gap, but only because his old man had decided in his own head that that's the way it was. Actually, Bordy thought his feelings about cops were probably very close to his old man's feelings about them: It was nice to know the cops were there when you needed them; otherwise, the less you had to do with them the better—for normal times, that was. Right at the moment he was very allergic to cops, and he realized it wouldn't get any better until he had unloaded that ring.

Suddenly too restless to stay home, he drove over to Jim McBride's. Jim suggested they go up to the Triangle Bar and shoot a game of pool.

"There'll be a list a mile long," Bordy said. "You wanta shoot pool, let's go to the Youth Center."

"*Youth* Center?" Jim had turned eighteen two weeks ago, and it was obvious his Youth-Center days were already far behind him.

The Triangle Bar was the main hangout for the young beer-drinking crowd on Nantasket Beach, and as usual it was jammed. There was only one pool table, with a list of a dozen names waiting to play. Jim added his and Bordy's.

"It'll take three hours before our turn comes up," Bordy said.

"What have we got to lose?" Jim pushed his way to the bar, came back with two bottles of Schlitz. "You gone sour on the world or something?" He peered at Bordy through his thick glasses. "You act like you're about forty years old tonight."

"Maybe it's a full moon."

"Hey, there's a couple seats!" Jim slid into one newly vacated chair, beckoned Bordy to the other.

Bordy sat down, realized there was another couple at the table, started to say, "Okay if we—" and stopped as if paralyzed by a poison dart. Mouth hanging open, he started straight into the eyes of Tabitha Saunders.

She gave him a polite little smile.

"Well, well! Pleasant surprise!" This from the guy seated next to him, across from Tabitha. Paul Eriksen, the Yalie.

Bordy's lost wits came straggling back and he made clumsy introductions. Jim McBride and Paul Eriksen immediately found a common interest—sound systems —and started gabbing away about quadraphonics and bass responses. Bordy had no interest but kept a smile on his face and pretended to listen. He couldn't keep his eyes off Tabitha. She looked absolutely great . . . sun-tanned, sparkling, blond hair a mass of soft, careless curls. She met his glance just once, and then directed her attention back to Paul. Bordy felt a pressure in his chest. He tried to drink his beer. Each swallow was like a solid lump all the way from his throat to his stomach.

Oh, boy. This was no good. He was not going to get hooked on Tabitha Saunders. No way. She was a rich kid and she had her Yalie boyfriend. There was absolutely no way he was going to get hooked on somebody like her.

Time dragged by. Paul Eriksen ordered another round of beers. Bordy didn't really want one, but he was in a peculiar state where he couldn't seem to get his jaw unlocked. Now Paul was talking about a rock concert he'd been to. His voice was loud, fast, a little slurry. Bordy looked at him, saw the flushed face, the glassy bright eyes. Paul Eriksen was getting drunk, and it couldn't have been from just a few beers.

He noticed that Tabitha hadn't touched her second beer. She was twirling her glass in her fingers, frowning at it. He wanted to say something to her but couldn't think of anything. Just then she looked up, met his eye, stared at him impassively for two or three seconds, look back down at her glass again.

"Been out in any more boats lately?" he blurted.

She shook her head, not looking at him. He felt totally stupid. Jim and Paul were still buzzing on their private line, Paul doing most of the talking, Jim listening with a happy dazed grin on his face. Just sitting in this bar, drinking beer, yakking with a guy from

Yale . . . right now that was a big-enough time for Jim. And Bordy for the first time in his life felt a flash of the difference between young and not so young. I don't believe it, he thought. Here I am eighteen years old, and all of a sudden this beer-drinking scene seems like kid stuff.

Busy with his own thoughts he didn't notice for a while what was happening at the table. When he tuned in again he heard Paul Eriksen saying, "This is very fine dope. Direct delivery from Jamaica."

For a second it didn't register. Paul Eriksen was lighting a cigarette. Cigarette, hell!

"Are you *nuts?* You can't smoke in here!"

"My dear chap . . ." Paul Eriksen took a long drag, held the smoke in his lungs, stared at Bordy with a silly, pop-eyed look. Then he stretched his arm across the table, offering the joint to Jim McBride, who shook his head and started looking around the room, probably for an escape hatch.

"Get rid of that damn thing!" Bordy said in a screaming whisper. "The owner'll call the cops. She's death on grass."

Paul Eriksen took another drag, gave him a goofy smile. His eyes were bright, and blank. Two tokes on top of whatever he'd been drinking had sent him instantly over the line.

"Hey, man, that smells like good stuff!" came a voice from the next table.

Bordy knew it was time to get out of there. The whole Park was full of Metropolitan District cops, and the Triangle Bar was absolutely one of the worst places in the world to try to smoke dope.

"You know what I told you, Paul!" Tabitha was on her feet, face pale and set. Bordy started to get up too. And then, with a shock he saw the plastic sandwich bag in the middle of the table. Looked like it had three or four more joints in it. He reached out, grabbed the bag, thrust it at Paul Eriksen.

"Here! Get this outa sight!"

But Paul was sitting there helpless, arms dangling at his sides, gone for all practical purposes from the land of the living.

"I'll just take that!" A voice in Bordy's ear; a firm hand gripping his arm above the elbow.

He whirled—and confronted a bearded stranger.

"I'm a police officer." The stranger took the bag from Bordy's suddenly numb fingers. "You're under arrest. It's my duty to inform you that anything you say may be used against you and that you have a constitutional right to remain silent or confer with your lawyer before you make any statement. That also goes for the rest of you." He looked at Tabitha and Jim and Paul. "You're all under arrest."

"For *what?*" Tabitha was definitely not intimidated.

"Possession of marijuana." He gave her a pleasant smile. "I'm arresting you on information. If you're clean you've got nothing to worry about. Meantime you'll have to come down to the station till we get it sorted out."

Bordy's brain was coming slowly unfrozen. He was standing in a pool of silence, surrounded by a banked ring of faces. It was like something straight out of TV. The undercover cop making the bust in the crowded bar. All they needed now was the big fight scene with three or four bodies flying through windows.

"Hey, look," he said. "That's not my dope."

"Save it till we get to the station," the cop said. "Let's go."

At the command, Paul stood up. "Whatever you say, Officer." He looked suddenly as sober as any well-known deacon.

So out of the bar they went, a peaceful little group, with the undercover cop bringing up the rear. When they hit the sidewalk he shepherded them quickly around the corner, away from the beach. There was a police van waiting, its blue light flashing a very bad message. How had it gotten there so fast?

But it didn't matter how. It was there, and then they were inside it, all five of them, nobody talking . . . the whole night, the whole life really, narrowing down to this rotten moment, sitting in the dark on hard benches wondering what was going to happen next.

At the station everything was businesslike, impersonal. They were lined up in front of a high counter, told to empty their pockets. All but Tabitha. A uniformed policewoman appeared and led her away, down a hall. Jim McBride was standing next to Bordy. As he laid his billfold on the counter his hand was trembling. Poor Jim. Of the four of them he was the most absolutely innocent. Paul Eriksen was standing aloof and composed, silently denying any connection whatsoever with Bordy or Jim.

Bordy put his wallet on the counter. Handkerchief and comb. Then his keys and some change. He reached in his other pocket. . . . *Oh, God, no!* He couldn't put that on the counter!

"Everything out of your pockets," the police sergeant behind the counter said.

Bordy looked up. The sergeant was staring directly at him. Bordy pulled out the envelope and laid it beside his wallet.

The sergeant started stuffing Paul Eriksen's belongings into a big brown envelope, listing everything as he went. Then he did the same for Jim, and then Bordy. When he picked up the white envelope he looked inside the torn end, then shook the envelope over his cupped hand. Out tumbled the diamond ring, flashing ten times brighter than all the lighthouses in Boston Harbor.

Bordy felt as though his stomach had fallen right out of his body. The sergeant peered at the ring, lifted a sharp curious eye, opened his mouth to speak, then for some reason of his own decided not to. He dropped the ring back in its envelope, put the white envelope into the brown envelope with the rest of Bordy's stuff, wrote down "One ring" on his list. And that was all.

Bordy couldn't believe it. He glanced sideways at Jim, who was staring straight ahead into his own agony. Paul Eriksen was contemplating his navel, or maybe his shoes. Amazingly, neither of them had noticed.

But it wasn't going to help, Bordy thought. He wasn't going to get away this easily. Before they were done, the police would want to know about the ring. How could he have been so stupid? Why was it in his pocket? He remembered now, though; he had gone straight to Myrtle Beame's house from the jewelers and had then completely forgotten that he had the ring in his pocket. It had been there when Steve McGovern came to the house and he hadn't thought about it even then. This day had been so long. Looking back at it, he felt as if it had begun about two weeks ago.

"All right, men." It was the plainclothes cop again. "Get your arms up. I'm going to have to pat you down." He made a good job of it, checking the linings of collars, the insides of belts, and then the total body area as though he suspected they might have something taped to their skins. Finally they had to take off their shoes and socks. It was embarrassing, and Bordy knew that if he hadn't felt so guilty he'd have felt a lot more indignant.

When it was over they were herded into another room where there was a man seated behind a desk; four chairs were lined up across from him, and Tabitha was sitting small and forlorn in one of them.

"This is Lieutenant James," their bearded escort said. "He wants to have a little talk with you."

Lieutenant James looked like your average TV police lieutenant: around forty, barbershop haircut, suit and tie, stern face.

"Sit down," he said.

They sat down. Bordy found himself between Jim McBride and Tabitha. He glanced at her. She gave him an unhappy smile.

"Who owns this stuff?" Lieutenant James dangled the little plastic bag between thumb and forefinger.

Nobody answered.

He dropped the bag on the desk top, let his eyes travel leisurely from face to face. He seemed unconcerned, almost bored. Bordy waited for the eyes to get to him. When they did he met them, willing his own eyes to be innocent and puzzled.

The lieutenant sighed, shook his head. "What I really want to know is where you got it. I'm not too interested in busting anybody for possession. I'm looking for the dealer." He paused, made a motion with his hand. "But I'll tell you this: if you don't come clean with me, I *will* book one of you." His finger jabbed sudden and sharp at Bordy. "Probably you."

"It's not my stuff!" The words popped out of him. He hadn't been able to think about what he was going to say, or not say. Compared to the ring, the grass had become unimportant. But now, suddenly and again, it was extremely important. The whole thing was so *nutty*. He couldn't make his mind work right.

"Whose is it?"

"It's not mine. That's all I know . . . it's not mine."

"That's all you know." The lieutenant looked at him, patiently, maybe sympathetically. "But you see, all I know is that you were holding this bag when Officer Donahue made the arrest. You had possession of the marijuana. And unless you give me a better reason to believe it wasn't yours . . ." He shrugged. "You're the one who's going to take the fall. What can I do?"

"It wasn't his!" Tabitha said, startling Bordy. "He just picked it up because it was on the table. I told you that."

"But how did it get on the table? That's what you didn't tell me." He looked up, frowning, at the bearded undercover cop who was standing off to one side. "Did you see anybody put this bag on the table, Donahue?"

"No, sir. When I came in I saw this man . . ." He pointed at Bordy. "I saw him pick up the bag. He was standing there, holding it."

"Was anybody smoking?"

"I didn't see anybody. Mrs. Tansey, the owner, told me this guy was smoking." He pointed at Paul. "And she thought they all were. But I didn't actually observe any of the subjects in the act of smoking."

"Great." The lieutenant leaned back in his chair, gazed at the ceiling. "So all we've got is four sticks of marijuana in the possession of . . ." He leaned forward, consulted a paper on his desk. "In the possession of Bordy Masterson." His eyes stabbed Bordy. "You don't look like a dealer to me. You don't even look like a user."

Bordy said nothing.

"But I'm going to book you, kid. Sure as hell I'm going to book you. Unless you tell me who put this grass on the table."

"Bordy didn't do it." Jim McBride's voice, with a quaver.

"Bordy didn't do it? Okay. That's three of you saying Bordy didn't do it. How about you?" The lieutenant looked at Paul Eriksen. "Do you think Bordy didn't do it?"

Paul didn't answer. Bordy looked over at him. He was slumped in his chair, staring straight ahead.

"Well, Mr. Eriksen?" The lieutenant's voice was gentle. "Who put the bag on the table?"

"I don't know." Paul Eriksen straightened himself in the chair, but his face hung slack. "I was drunk. I don't even remember what happened."

The lieutenant nodded impassively, rubbed the side of his jaw with his fingertips. "Do you know what the penalty for possession of marijuana is?" he asked, letting his eyes travel from face to face. "We're not one of those decriminalized states, you know. The penalty in Massachusetts, just for possession, is up to six months in jail. Now I'm not going to ask you again who brought that bag into the Triangle. I think I know who did it. But I honestly don't want to bust any one of you for possession. I'm after the pushers. So here's what I'm going to do. . . ." He paused for a long minute, as though making sure in his mind exactly what he *was* going to do.

"Tonight I'm going to let you go. I'll be in touch with you again in two days. And in the meantime I want you to think about what happened tonight. And I want the person who owned this grass to think very seriously about the kind of pressure that's on the other three. Because although I don't want to bust any of you, I'll have to do it, unless the guilty party lets me know where he got this grass. If he does, then you're all home free. If he doesn't, then one of you is going to get pinched. And you can figure out for yourselves who that's going to be."

Bordy sat very still, not meeting the lieutenant's eyes. He heard what was being said but didn't really understand it, couldn't concentrate on it.

"All right, you can go."

They all stood up.

"All but you." He pointed at Bordy. "You stick around a little while."

Bordy sat down.

"I'll wait outside," Jim said.

Bordy nodded. He didn't trust himself to speak. He was suddenly scared again, worse than ever. This police station was like a roller coaster. Every time you hit bottom and took a breath, they started hauling you up another hill.

When the others had gone the lieutenant said, "It's Eriksen, right?"

"I . . . Look, I don't want to talk about it right now."

"You'd rather spend the night in the cooler?"

"You said you were gonna let us go."

"Maybe I changed my mind."

Bordy swallowed, said nothing.

"Would you tell me why you'd want to take a rap for that jerk?"

Bordy shook his head. Inside him everything was knotting tighter and tighter. "I don't . . ." He stopped. "You said you'd give us two days."

"So I did." The lieutenant pushed his chair back from the desk. "Just don't be a sap. You understand?"

Bordy nodded, started to get up.

"Where'd you get that diamond ring?"

The question caught him completely off guard. He couldn't think. And knew with a breaking feeling inside him that he didn't want to think.

"It belongs to the woman I work for."

"How come you're carrying it around in your pocket?"

"I . . ." He was standing naked on that beach again. Covered with ice. But with no hope now . . . no possible hope now.

"Kid, I don't know about you," the lieutenant said, shaking his head. "You can call a lawyer if you want to, but I'd suggest you just tell me all about this ring."

chapter 14

He had heard about jail, sure. Had seen it in the movies and on the tube. But when he woke up to his first morning in jail he realized that nobody could ever tell anybody about jail. You couldn't even show anybody about jail. The only way you could know about jail was to be *in* jail. And that didn't mean walking around in a jail and looking at it. Because jail was a feeling. The only way you could feel it was to do it, or rather, have it done *to* you.

The jailer who brought him his lukewarm coffee and stale doughnuts hardly looked at him. That was part of the jail trip, too. Most of the cops weren't brutal or mean or even disapproving. They fed him and fingerprinted him and took his picture, always with an attitude of unconcern, almost disinterested, maybe the way a professional dog trainer would look after his animals. They talked about baseball and their wives and what they were going to do on their days off. They talked right through Bordy or around him as though he weren't there. It was a horrible feeling, as though he'd been set outside the human race somehow and was now being processed, maybe turned into dog meat or something.

In the afternoon his mother came and talked to him, in a small room, across a table, with Lieutenant James standing there, looking out a window, saying nothing. His mother didn't cry, didn't even say, How could you do this to us? She was quiet and scared and waiting for him to tell her something that would make it all right. She said she'd get him a lawyer, that his father didn't know yet, but it would be all right, they'd get him a lawyer. He said he didn't want a lawyer. He tried to tell her what had happened, but it was just too complicated. In the end he couldn't tell her anything, except that it was okay and he was okay and not to worry and a lot of stupid nothingness.

And then the next day the unbelievable happened. They let him out of jail. Lieutenant James walked with him down the long hall to the front door.

"Kid, you are one lucky kid. I hope you know that."

Bordy nodded. They had stopped just inside the door. He wanted to be gone, but on another level he was afraid of what lay outside that door. The past two days had been so bad he couldn't bear to look back on them. What lay ahead might in a different way be even worse.

"The old lady refused to press charges, would not believe you were going to steal that ring. She thinks you're a great kid."

Bordy was looking at the floor.

"Come on. Get your head up. That old lady isn't just giving you a break. She's a smart old lady. I don't mean smart . . . wise. You can't con that old lady. And she's got a faith in you. She told me there was no way you could ever have gone through with it." The lieutenant snorted through his nose. "I think she's wrong about that. But maybe it doesn't matter. She almost convinced me."

Slowly Bordy raised his eyes. There was a great hard lump in his throat.

"Your parents feel the same way. Which doesn't necessarily mean too much, seeing as they're your parents." He was looking at Bordy, straight-faced, but with a shadow of a grin in his eyes and the corners of his mouth. "And then . . . maybe what convinced me more . . . was your girl friend Tabitha and that guy McBride. They came to bat for you too, one thousand percent. They got that weasel Eriksen to give me the name of his dealer, which got you off the hook on the marijuana beef."

"She's . . . uh . . . she's not my girl friend," Bordy said, choking on the words.

"You got people like that who think you're okay," the lieutenant said, "you got something important going for you." He stuck out his hand. "I think you got something else going for you, too, Bordy. Just don't get in too big a hurry."

Bordy shook his hand and stumbled through the door into the afternoon sunlight. The glare was so bright it blinded him. He put his hand to his eyes. He was not going to cry.

"Bordy?"

It was Tabitha, standing by the curb.

"Grandma thought you might like to come over for a cup of coffee or something."

"Oh . . . I . . ." He stared at her. He couldn't talk.

"It's all right." Her face was very serious. "Why don't we go for a walk on the beach?"

"I was going to steal that ring."

"Let's go for a walk on the beach."

As he crossed the street beside her he felt the first small surge of hope, lifting him a little bit, like an unexpected sea swell. It was a very good feeling.